# THE
# TRIUMPH

## BOOKS BY GENE EDWARDS

A Tale of Three Kings
The Divine Romance
The Prisoner in the Third Cell
Revolution: The Story of the Early Church
The Inward Journey
The Highest Life
The Secret to the Christian Life
Letters to a Devastated Christian
What Happens When a Christian Dies
Climb the Hightest Mountain
Crucified by Christians
Our Mission
Overlooked Christianity
The Silas Diary

*The Chronicles of the Door*
The Beginning
The Escape
The Birth
The Triumph
The Return

# The Triumph

## THE CHRONICLES OF
## THE DOOR

# Gene Edwards

Tyndale House
Publishers, Inc.
Wheaton, Illinois

**Library of Congress Cataloging-in-Publication Data**

Edwards, Gene, date
  The triumph / Gene Edwards.
    p.   cm. — (The Chronicles of the door)
  ISBN 0-8423-6978-3
  1. Jesus Christ—Fiction.  2. Bible.  N.T.—History of Biblical
events—Fiction.  I. Title.  II. Series.
PS3555.D924T75   1995
813′.54—dc20                          94-23227

Printed in the United States of America

01  00
9   8   7   6   5

# PROLOGUE

"It is Michael. He is close to madness. Recorder, what shall we do?"

Recorder looked up into the panicked face of the angel Rathel.

"Then he has entered the temple grounds? He has heard the plot against his Lord?" replied the recording angel.

"Yes, and if they lay hands on the Lord, I fear Michael will act without command. If he does, a third of heaven's host *must go* with him. Disobedience will once more mar the heavenlies.

"Recorder, you know Michael well. His Lord is in grave danger, yet Michael has been allowed to do nothing. Seeing his Lord in danger, yet not allowed to take action, is something Michael simply cannot understand."

As Rathel expected, Recorder's answer did not come quickly.

"At the last moment, if all else fails, I will stand before Michael," replied Recorder. "But it may be a futile gesture. We are speaking of Michael, the one created to be *the avenging angel*. Tonight there is much to avenge. To expect him to deny that fierce nature of his—given to him by God himself—is perhaps expecting too much of Michael. Fallen men plot dark deeds against the Son of God. Should those plots become deeds, it may be more than our comrade can endure."

Recorder sighed, then continued.

"Tell Gabriel to withstrain Michael as long as possible. Should the moment come when all else has failed . . . if Michael orders his charge to follow him through the Door, then . . . but not before, *call me forth.*"

"Will he listen to you, Recorder?"

"I know many things, but this I do not know," replied Recorder gloomily.

For a long moment Rathel stared at the most mysterious of all the angels, then dared to venture his question again, slightly changed. "Can Recorder stop Michael?"

"I am not sure."

"Is it within the confines of the possible?" persisted an adamant Rathel.

"Who, or what, can restrain Michael from protecting his Lord? Can Michael be helped to comprehend such matters?"

"Then we are doomed?"

For a moment Recorder surveyed his inmost wisdom, then let out a painful sigh.

"Rathel, it is not within my duties and privileges to know." Those words were followed by a flash of anger. "But this is," he added abruptly: "Rathel, find your duty."

With that Rathel vanished, reappearing at Gabriel's side.

# PART

# I

# CHAPTER
## *One*

"Judas. Has he arrived?"

The words belonged to Caiaphas, the high priest.

"Within the hour, sir."

"The guards?"

"Yes. The Romans have consented to go with us. They have their swords. The temple guards are armed with clubs and staves."

"Judas has warned us that his disciples may resist. Prevent them by any means. Kill if you must. The lunatic must be in chains, tonight. What of the witnesses?"

"They are here."

"Have they been told what to say?"

"As we speak."

"When Judas arrives, go with him immediately. Are there torches?"

"Yes, and lamps."

"Judas will kiss the Nazarene—no one else. Extend no graciousness to this heretic. Bind him immediately."

Caiaphas, turning to reenter his house, paused and

inquired again. "Have all in the Sanhedrin been notified?"

"Yes. Most are on their way here."

Words spoken in whisper are often overheard in the most surprising of places. On this particular occasion the words of Caiaphas, uttered to a few scribes and priests, resounded clearly in the ears of a very imposing archangel who was standing close by.

"Never in time nor eternity will you bind my Lord," vowed the outraged Michael. "You shall not so much as touch him. You will surely not put the Lord of glory on trial. If you try, you will deal with more than earthly followers. You will deal with me, and legions of livid angels."

With these words spoken but unheard Michael vanished, only to reappear in a nearby garden named Gethsemane.

# CHAPTER
## *Two*

"Ironsmith?"

"That is correct."

"We have two thieves and an insurrectionist to crucify on the morrow. We will have need of nails before noon. Can you comply?"

"I can."

"Then forge a good supply, for if the Sanhedrin has its way, there may be a fourth."

"Another thief?" inquired the smith.

"No, a Galilean. The one all those people held a parade for last week. Do you know of him?"

"I do."

"We will also need three, perhaps four, cross-beams. I understand you can also provide these?"

"The patibula? Yes. I make them from cypress wood, six feet long, five inches thick, and ten inches high, as Romans measure. Each will weigh about fifty pounds."

"Hew four."

"Do you also need four stipes cructs?"

"No, I think not. There are many stakes still in

place on the hill. Or, perhaps, tomorrow we will simply use a tree. I will return at dawn. Have them ready."

With those words the centurion departed.

The smith furrowed his brow as he contemplated what he was about to do.

"The Galilean? Indeed, I have heard of him! If he truly be God, what terrible thing am I about to do? Shall I take out from the earth the ore that he planted there at creation? With that ore shall I fashion nails to crucify earth's Creator? If he be God, shall I fashion from the forest, which he created, a crossbeam upon which to crucify him?

"Shall the hands that placed iron deep in the bowels of earth clutch bloodstained nails on a cross? Shall his feet, which once tread Orion's paths, tomorrow tread the winepress alone? Shall the one who called out in the darkness 'Let there be light' be taken as a common criminal, in the darkness of this foreboding night?

"If he be God, then this is the most dreadful of all hours."

# CHAPTER
## *Three*

"Gabriel, will our Lord be safe this night in the shelter of that garden?" asked an anxious Rathel.

"Where is Michael?" replied an equally anxious Gabriel.

"He has been in the court of Caiaphas. Presently he stands at the edge of the garden. I must tell you, in the courtyard of Caiaphas, men are gathering with swords and clubs. False witnesses are being told what to say. They plan to take our Lord by Judas's greeting. I fear that Judas knows where our Lord is and will take them there."

"What of the eleven?"

"They are in Gethsemane with the Lord. But they are asleep."

"What!" exclaimed the astounded archangel. "His followers—asleep? On such a perilous night?

"But why am I surprised?" continued Gabriel. "The recording angel warned us of an hour such as this. Nor is it really sleeping followers that troubles me."

"Then?"

"There is *so much* Mystery . . . so much we who are spirit beings cannot fathom. Of this night I, for one, know nothing. Our Lord, clothed in human vestige, deep in troubled conversation with his Father, his words so grave, his humanity so evident."

"He seems so vulnerable," was Rathel's ponderous reply. "He is groaning and weeping, not as men might normally weep, but as no mortal ever has. *Never* has one of the race of Adam been in such agony. It is the most terrifying thing I have ever beheld. His words clutched at the very depths of my spirit. Can the human body long bear such sorrow? I think not. If there is no relief soon, his heart will surely burst asunder. Is it possible, Gabriel? Can human sorrow plunge to so great a depth?"

"Perhaps we should visit the garden. Michael also concerns me."

Slipping first past eight sleeping figures, then three more, the two messengers moved near the center of the garden.

"It is far worse than before," murmured Rathel. "He cannot long survive this agony of soul."

"Nor is there any encouragement in seeing Michael. Look at him."

"I have never seen him like this," added Rathel, shuddering.

Michael, standing not far from his Lord, was speaking almost incoherently.

"His face. See his face," muttered Michael. "His face. His body is pouring forth, not sweat, but . . .

*blood!* Something must be done. Now. Or he will breathe his last."

Michael turned toward his two celestial companions, his glazed eyes dancing with fire.

"Gabriel, Rathel, it is time to act. Return to our realm. Call forth the angels in your charge, Gabriel, and mine also. Ready them for battle. I will remain here to do the unspeakable. I must minister to him who is the very ministry of my life. I must comfort him who is Comfort."

Gabriel, not at all surprised at Michael's words, yet fearful of their outcome, hesitated, then vanished. Rathel considered saying something, but seeing the depth of rage on Michael's face, stepped silently back into the other realm.

Michael moved closer to the prostrate body of his Lord. Slowly, reverently, Michael cradled the head of Jesus in his mighty arms.

"Rest your head on mine, my Lord. Breathe deeply. Cease your tears. I hold you. There is nothing to fear. The legions of heaven await your command. No harm shall befall you, my Sovereign."

Taking his own spotless garment of light in his hands, the archangel began wiping the blood from the face of the Author of Creation, while Michael's tears mingled with the blood of his Lord.

"Breathe deep of winds unseen. Fear no man. Lord, a hundred million swords await your bidding."

The Lord raised his head and studied the face of Michael.

"It is not man I fear, old friend. Nor angels, nor demons, nor impatient Death. Go, Michael, leave me here. My Father and I, we must . . . Michael, return to realms unseen. Await my call."

For a moment longer the Carpenter clutched Michael's garments. Upon releasing them, Michael knew that his time to depart must be delayed no longer. Nonetheless, beholding the blood-drenched face of the Son of God was driving him closer to insanity.

"Await my command, Michael," repeated the Carpenter. "Do nothing unless I so order. Do you understand, Michael? Whatever happens . . . nothing."

Michael's weeping turned to uncontrollable sobs as he again pressed his Lord against his bosom.

"My Lord and my God, what hour is this?"

"Return to our realm, highest of all archangels. Await my call."

There was a noise. Michael turned. One of the disciples, John by name, struggled to pull himself free of sleep. In that instant Michael disappeared. John fell back to sleep.

# CHAPTER
## *Four*

"Father, it is not the whip I fear. Nor the nails, nor the crowd's derision. Not even my enemy, Death. It is the cup—and the dark draught that lies within. Father, you have never been apart from me. We are one. Forever we are one. That tomorrow we might not be one is a thought worse than a thousand Sheols.

"Father, the cup. Please withhold it . . . if there be any other course, find it now. If it is possible, let it not enter me."

Jesus began shaking violently as he considered offering a prayer he dared not pray. The struggle between the will of the Father and the will of the Son intensified.

Finally, there rose from the lips of the Carpenter a prayer that brought him perilously close to accepting the horror that would come to him should he embrace his Father's will.

"Father, show me . . . the contents . . . show me what lies within that bitter cup!"

The garden suddenly grew ghastly dark. The stars

disappeared. Space, time, and matter vanished. A vile stench wafted across the eerie 'scape.

Jesus groaned, "Come infernal cup. Show me thy iniquitous brew."

There began to emerge before him who is all purity, a cup of all impurities, spewing with every decadent deed, defilement, and vileness the race of fallen man had ever executed.

*All that is unforgivable*
*all that is unpardonable*
*all that is depraved*
*All nefarious malfeasance of creation*
*I must look upon thy filth*
*ere I partake of thee.*

The execrable potion moved closer to the Christ, still spewing its foul stench and deviate brew.

Jesus, shaking violently, blood pouring from every pore, groaned, then continued his agonizing prayer.

"O Father, in the vast recesses of the past, in time before time, even in ages before the eternals, we cast forth a plan that awed even divinity. Then I fashioned the stars and founded the nebulae and placed into the heavens its fiery comets, as creation spun forth from my hand and reflected in my eyes.

"Even as I was slain there, creation was birthed.

"I came as earth's wheat, to die, then to come forth many seed, as Life. Life to be begotten in man. But, O my God, the depravity infused within that cup.

Must it be? O Father, forget not I now live in frail humanity, and there is added to me the soul's own will."

From out of the depth of a heart's shredded anguish, the Carpenter continued to offer up petitions of such travail that only groans could give them utterance.

"Father, the cup that lies before me is all the violations of all history in all places, while the defiling deeds committed by men even in this hour add their bile into this felonious brew."

With those words, the cup spewed anew as it received again the venomous fomentations of depraved mankind.

The Son of God began to weep, his tears joined by those of his Father.

> *Where never I have sown,*
> *there must I reap.*
> *The damnations of Adam's breed*
> *must I drink.*

"Father, I have never . . . never . . ." He groaned as he stared at the repulsive scene. "Father, it is all unholy. O Father, unholy as is the cup, unholy its makers. Father, I am holy, as you are holy. Is there no other way for them to become righteous as you are righteous . . . except the cup?

"Except I *become* the cup!"

The Carpenter's voice strengthened!

His will yielded.

"That they might be one. As we . . .

"O Father. For that, permit even this!"

Heaven trembled. Hell shook. Jesus rose, his face toward a hill outside Jerusalem.

An unsteady hand reached down and shook Peter. "Awaken James and John," came the trembling voice.

The three men stirred, then slowly, sheepishly climbed to their feet.

"In the name of God, who are you?" asked a terrified Peter as he looked up.

Peter rammed his fist into his mouth as he recognized the tragic figure standing before him. "My Lord, it is you! What has happened? You are covered with blood. You look more dead than alive!"

James and John joined Peter in horrid awe as they looked upon him who had this night won forever the title, *Man of Sorrows*. The face of the Nazarene was streaked with blood, his hair caked in sweat and blood, his garments glistening red, his countenance virtually indiscernible.

"Come," replied the Carpenter, ignoring the shock etched on the faces of his disciples. The three men hesitated. It was not easy to follow someone hardly recognizable as a man.

John first moved forward, driven by a question he had to ask.

"Lord, I dreamed. I dreamed I saw an angel. He was ministering to you, then he disappeared. Did I see this or was it but a dream?"

"Follow me, John. The cup that my Father has given me, shall I not soon drink it?"

A frail Lord, more vulnerable than ever the disciples had seen him, staggered on toward his other sleeping followers.

A moment later they, too, were struggling to their feet, and like the three, stared aghast at the sight of their Master.

There was a noise. All heads turned. Someone was approaching.

"Who could be coming here at this hour?" whispered Peter. Then, attempting to regain some credibility, he reached clumsily for a sword that he had hidden beneath his garments.

"John Mark! What are you doing here?" came the scolding voice of James. "You belong at home, in bed. No ten year old ought to be out this late."

"I could not sleep. No one in the house can. I was afraid, and . . ." John Mark dropped his head. ". . . and I was curious.

"But listen to me! On my way here I passed through the center of the city. Near the temple . . . there are guards everywhere! I watched and listened. I think they are coming here!"

Eleven men looked toward the city. In the distance could be seen torches and lanterns that, true enough, seemed to be moving toward the Garden of Gethsemane.

# CHAPTER
## *Six*

"Is the night playing tricks on my eyes? It looks like hundreds of them," wondered the Levite aloud.

"Perhaps there are even more of them than it appears," muttered Thomas. "It takes many a lantern to light the night that brightly."

"Look. Judas. He is coming this way. Perhaps he can tell us what is happening," observed Thaddeus.

"Judas? I thought he was here with us," came Peter's surprised response.

At that moment, leaving his disciples behind him, the Lord began walking swiftly toward Judas.

"Judas!" called out Jesus in a clear voice.

Judas hesitated. Uncertain, he raised a torch and squinted his eyes to better see the face of the one who had called to him.

"Master? Is it you?" responded Judas as he stared at the emaciated face of the Teacher.

Certain now it was Jesus, Judas moved forward and kissed the Lord on the cheek.

"Betrayal, by means of a kiss," whispered the Carpenter. "Father, permit even this."

By now the mob following Judas had come into full view. There were hundreds in its ranks, the captain of the temple guard in the lead, the soldiers who protect the scribes and those assigned to protect the high priests following close on. Behind them were scores of other men carrying clubs.

Spying an army of this size, the disciples hesitated.

Jesus now moved past Judas toward the belligerent throng.

"Who is that half-dead wretch," asked the captain of the guard, "and why has Judas not signaled to us which of those men is the Nazarene?"

"Whom do you seek?" came the certained voice of the Carpenter, now almost face-to-face with the guardsman.

The captain's words were gruff and loud, spoken that they might be clearly heard by the eleven disciples standing in the distance. "We seek Jesus of Nazareth," he responded, even as he walked past the blood-soaked Carpenter.

"I am Jesus, whom you seek."

The captain whirled about, and in so doing stumbled and fell. As he did, he carried others of the startled men with him. After a moment of ensuing confusion and no small amount of fear, the captain was back on his feet and facing the man who had spoken.

"*Who* are *you?*" he asked, his words still betraying uncertainty.

"I am Jesus, whom you seek."

With that answer the captain found his voice and his courage.

"Bind him."

Hearing those very unacceptable words, an angry archangel named Michael and an angry man named Peter lunged forward.

# CHAPTER
## *Seven*

Peter drew his sword and raced toward the mob. "Is it time for battle and the sword, Lord?" exclaimed an adamant Peter, swinging his sword wildly over his head as he rushed forward. At that same moment the mighty hand of Michael, with far more certainty, reached for his sword.

Jesus was about to give answer to Peter's question when Peter's sword struck the ear of a slave named Malchus. Several men in the mob grabbed at Peter. As they did, the largest sword in creation came fully unsheathed, but not before the words of the Carpenter reached the ears of both sword-bearers.

"If I needed protection, I would be furnished with more than twelve legions of sword-drawn angels," cried the Lord in a loud, clear voice. "But this is not that hour. It is not mine to call forth the angels of my Father. Rather, it is for me to drink the cup that my Father has given me."

An ill-tempered Peter and an even more provoked archangel hesitated.

Jesus paused, then whispered words uttered so softly that only celestial ears could hear.

"Not swords, nor battle, nor angels, Michael. Only a cup."

The Carpenter raised himself to his full height and shattered the strange gloom of that strange night with a voice that trumpeted across the garden.

"The thieves that you arrested, have you confused me with them? You have seen me before. Every day, in the temple. Yet, look at you. You come out to me as though I were a robber? I have been in your temple every day, including *this* day, speaking openly."

Jesus looked straight into the faces of the leading priests. "You did not arrest me nor even stretch out your hand against me. Not then. The reason you did not? It is because your time had not come. What you are doing now, you do only because it has been allowed you by my Father."

Full-throated, the Lord cried out again with words addressed to the darkened hearts of treacherous men and to the ears of those in the unseen realm of darkness.

"This is your hour!"

"To whom is he speaking?" questioned Michael. "Whose hour is this? Is this the hour of Lucifer?" he snarled.

Gabriel was instantly at Michael's side, capturing Michael's right hand as he spoke.

"You must understand, this is not *my* hour nor

*yours*, Michael," declared a determined Gabriel. "This is *not* the hour of elect angels. Everything has changed. The balance has shifted. Michael, you must understand, your Lord has accepted that cup which so horrified him."

Michael fisted his hand before his face and cried, "Oh, dear Lord, please say the word, then will more than twelve legions of enraged angels come to rescue you."

The Lord's response was immediate, though his words were addressed, not to Michael nor to the transfixed mob, but to the citizenry of evil.

"Darkness, you have your power. You and your powers are, as of this moment, set free. Divine restraint is lifted. *Now* is your hour. This is the hour of the powers of darkness. *Do what you may!*"

As commanded by some unseen force, the mob encircling Jesus suddenly found its courage and grabbed the Carpenter. Quickly they bound his hands while eleven terrified men and one young boy fled into the night.

Two youths in the crowd noted the size and speed of the fleeing boy. Marking him as their prey, they ran after him, soon grabbing John Mark's garment and pulling on it furiously. John Mark, frantic, turned and began running backward, managing to pull free of his captured cloak. Whirling around again, he fled naked toward Jerusalem and home.

With Gabriel's prodding, a bewildered Michael stepped reluctantly through the Door separating the two realms. Jesus was alone in a world now wholly governed by darkness. The Carpenter found himself in the most dangerous of all possible places. He was in the hands of religious men.

"Take him to the old one. To Annas. He knows better than anyone the formalities to be followed."

It was 3:00 A.M.

# CHAPTER
## *Eight*

Michael's return to the heavenlies brought consternation to the entire heavenly host. In dumbfounded
silence the heavenly host pushed back in horror as
Michael staggered toward them.

"The blood of a man on the garments of an archangel!" cried Adorae, aghast at what he saw. "What
has happened to the avenger? It is as though he has
fought with Death. From whence comes this
blood?!"

"From our Lord?" cried the inner voice of Rathel.

Michael's eyes were blurred, his face gaunt and
formless. The mightiest hands in the created universe were trembling violently. Seeing the horrified
stares of the heavenly host, Michael looked down at
his hands and raiment.

"It is the blood—"

Michael's voice broke. Shaking uncontrollably, the
archangel covered his face with his hands, trying to
vanquish the terrible memory that passed across the
mind of his spirit.

"It is the blood . . ." Michael clenched his eyes

with his fists while the light of his being flashed intermittently.

"... 'Tis the blood of my Lord," screamed Michael, finally succumbing to hysteria.

The horrified host of heaven groaned in agony, the scene too painful to bear.

"The blood of our Lord on the vestments of Michael," observed Rathel. Not one angel moved.

Michael began speaking to no one in particular.

"There is danger everywhere. It hangs inexorably in the air and penetrates the inmost being. This is the dreaded hour, and there is nothing I can do. Do you understand? *Nothing* I can do. The night is so dark. So dark."

Just for an instant Michael seemed to throw off his delirium. Searching about him with eyes that could hardly see, he asked wildly, "Is Gabriel here?"

"I am here, Michael, beside you, as are my charge."

"And mine?" responded a groping Michael. "My charge, are they here?"

"They, too, are here."

"I must take no action. Not on my command, but upon his alone."

Rathel's taut body eased. Sighs of relief were heard through all the arrayed host.

"One rebellion in heaven's history is enough," whispered Gloir.

But the hopes of Gloir, Rathel, and the entire host were suddenly dashed. Michael had turned back toward the garden scene.

# CHAPTER
## *Nine*

As a precaution, the captain of the guard led the criminal back into Jerusalem by a circuitous route.

Pharisees, Levites, temple priests, temple guards, and the Roman legionnaires, led by one called a chiliarch, marched the prisoner north until they were past the city; then, dropping down, they entered Jerusalem from the west. In a moment they were on Caesar's territory, the Antonia Fortress, a fortress manned by Syrian-born soldiers enlisted in Caesar's army.

"Where is the magician to be taken from here?" asked the chiliarch.

"To the Maccabean Palace. The grand Sanhedrin is convening there to try him."

The temple guards ushered the prisoner out of the fortress area, past Herod's palace, and toward a large double courtyard that fronted the Maccabean Palace, the palatial homes of Annas and Caiaphas.

Seeing Jesus being led in, all those in the courtyard immediately converged before the home of the high priest, while at the same time staring at the emaciated figure standing at the courtyard's center.

"It is him."

"They have done it! He is ours!"

"He looks grotesque."

"I would not have recognized him."

"Guard well the gate. He has friends."

"Take him to the ancient one. Annas should be the first to question this man."

Annas was the oldest living man who had served as high priest. Such a standing caused him to be considered wise. He was also powerful.

"The witnesses, call the witnesses," whispered Caiaphas.

Annas emerged from his house. "Do not allow the blasphemer inside my home," came the shrill voice of Annas.

Walking slowly toward the prisoner, Annas studied Jesus' face. *It will be a short walk to death for this one,* he thought. *He is already half dead.*

Annas placed his face before the Carpenter.

"Why do you teach treachery, sedition, and heresy? And who follows you?"

"Question those who have heard me," replied Jesus. "All who have heard me know what it is I teach."

Those words hardly out of Jesus' mouth, a temple guard struck his face with his fist.

"You are speaking to the high priest, and *that* is no way to speak to the high priest."

The guard did not know it, but by that act he had pushed an archangel very near to the edge. Until now the strong arm of Gabriel had managed to restrain Michael. Nonetheless, Michael's lucidity was deteriorating rapidly. Gabriel, as well as all the elect angels, knew the next such incident would send Michael out of control.

Annas motioned to Caiaphas. The man presently reigning as high priest now took over the inquisition.

The interrogation had gone on for over an hour. Nothing was going as it should. Caiaphas was desperate and almost frantic.

Annas slipped up beside Caiaphas and whispered hoarsely. "We will never convince Pilate he should allow us to put this one to death with what you have so far."

"What can I do?" shot back Caiaphas angrily. "Can I be blamed if the witnesses cannot keep their stories together?"

"There is one other thing you can do."

"What?" replied a frustrated Caiaphas.

"Adjure."

"Yes! Of course. Why not? But what if he lies?"

Annas's words struck like an arrow into the hearts of both men. "This man does not lie."

Caiaphas gathered up his blue-and-white garments and walked back to the center of the courtyard and to his intended victim. "I adjure you by the Living God, are you the Messiah? Are you the Son of God?"

The Lord looked slowly around the courtyard, studying the faces of scores of priests, rabbis, scribes, and Pharisees. He then looked toward Annas and the guard. Finally he raised his eyes toward the horizon to discover what human eyes could not see. Upon the roof of every house that surrounded the courtyard, and beyond to the hills and reaching out to the fields beyond Jerusalem, stood thousands of vigilant angels.

Finally the Carpenter's eyes met those of an archangel. The face of Michael was a river of glistening tears.

Exalta eased himself over to Gloir. "He is going to say it, is he not? I never dreamed he would allow the ears of fallen men to hear him acknowledge the ends of truth."

"It will cost him everything," responded Gloir. "What shall we do?"

"Nothing beyond what we are allowed to do."

Very gently, almost imperceptibly, the Lord gazed at his unseen guardian, and finally to the high priest.

Jesus leaned into the face of Caiaphas and with a calmness that seemed to shake the very ground beneath Jerusalem, he replied.

*I Am.*

Having uttered those words, he once more looked toward Michael and then continued. "Furthermore, *a day is coming* when you will see the Son of Man returning with his angels upon a cloud of glory."

"Lord, hasten that hour," whispered the archangel.

Caiaphas had hoped for such words to fall from the lips of the Carpenter. Just in case he won such an acknowledgment, Caiaphas had already planned what he would do. In mock rage he clutched at his garments and, tearing them, began to scream.

"Who needs witnesses! We have heard this Galilean blaspheme *our* God. He has done so with his own mouth . . . here . . . even in the presence of the Sanhedrin. This man has witnessed to his own heresy.

"I call for a vote of the Sanhedrin."

Caiaphas stepped back and pointed his hand directly toward Jesus. "I know my decision. This Nazarene is not worthy to live. Cast your vote. If loyalty to God is in you, it will be as mine. If God be with us, we shall see him dead before the Passover begins."

"Noooo!" cried Michael as once more he reached to unsheathe his sword. Once more Gabriel restrained him. Once more Michael yielded strength to sovereignty.

An unmistakable voice sounded inside the spirits of both archangels. "Return to the heavenlies."

The host of heaven turned and reluctantly stepped back into their own realm. The last and most reluctant of all was Michael.

It was 5:00 A.M.

# CHAPTER
## *Eleven*

While the Sanhedrin cast their vote, and while Caiaphas plotted his next move, a new scene was unfolding in Jerusalem.

One of the temple priests climbed the temple walls
until at last he stood on top of one of the pinnacles
of the temple. Facing east he searched the horizon
intently, while the temple courtyard below, choked
with pilgrims pushing their way through the
twenty-four entrances into the temple grounds,
watched anxiously.

The priest carefully studied the landscape. Just
beyond the city lay the slopes of the Mount of
Olives, and across the open fields, the road leading
out of Bethany. A trickle of faithful Hebrews could be
seen making their way toward the East Gate.

For a moment the priest turned to observe the
opposite side of the city. Pilgrims coming up from
the Joppa road were pouring into Jerusalem from the
western gates.

At that moment the tip of the sun appeared over
the eastern hills.

The priest cried out to those below: "The morning sun!"

From below, another priest inquired as to how far a distance could the morning light be seen.

"Even to Hebron?" came the traditional question.

"Yes," he cried in return. "Even to Hebron!"

The crowd below began to applaud.

It was 5:45 A.M.

Suddenly temple priests appeared all along the walls of the city, raising long trumpets. In a moment the air was filled with the loud blasts of silver horns.

The pilgrims cheered again, while the more jaded citizens of Jerusalem, still in bed, received the sounds of the trumpets simply as a call to rise to a new day. Such locals would probably make no effort to reach the temple courtyard until afternoon.

As the trumpet blasts receded, some fifty priests, each assigned to specific chores, began their duties.

The responsibility of a few of these men was to sacrifice a lamb at this particular moment. This sacrifice, unlike the lamb to be slaughtered late in the evening, was a daily routine carried out every morning at the rising of the sun.

Outside the temple, women began scurrying to one temple court as the men moved toward another. The morning sacrifice of a lamb and the morning prayer would be offered to God simultaneously.

The lamb was led to a gold bowl, where it drank water, and was then led to the altar.

At that same moment the hands of Jesus were tied.

Now bound, he stood in the Maccabean courtyard awaiting the result of the Sanhedrin vote, even as the right forefoot of the lamb was tied to its right hind-foot. An iron ring attached to the altar was then placed over the head of the lamb, and its face turned toward the west. The incense altar was lit, the seven candles of the lampstand trimmed. In a moment the lamb was dead.

The voting was finished. Jesus was found guilty.

Then came the sentencing. The Sanhedrin had decided that, by Hebrew law, the Carpenter was to die.

It was 6:00 A.M. In twelve hours the Sabbath would begin. If Jesus was to die before 6:00 P.M., these men had to hurry.

"As you all have witnessed, we heard this man speak *gillupha*. He blasphemed. Now take this blas-phemer away. He is not worthy to live. Such is the will of the Sanhedrin."

Gabriel's hand tightened on Michael's arm.

39

# CHAPTER
## *Twelve*

"Beat him. When you have finished with the whipping, make sure he looks like the monster that he is. Then take him to Pilate. I want no pity for this man coming from Pilate. I mean for this Galilean to die before the Passover. Do what must be done."

Before men and angels, the crack of the soldier's whip resounded through the halls of judgment.

Little could those present know that whip's lash had sent a deranged and screaming Michael past all restraint. Gabriel pitted his own mighty arm against Michael's. Another crack of the cruel lash resounded through the Door. All angelic eyes turned toward Michael.

*Let not this hour become as was the great rebellion,* pled Gloir to himself. But even as these words crossed his spirit, his eyes told him that Michael had gone beyond the breaking point. Legions of angels were now under the command of one who teetered on the edge of insanity. Dread was on every face and tears in many eyes.

There was another crack of the whip. It found its

mark on the back of the Carpenter. Pressed beyond his call, pressed beyond control, the mightiest archangel of all, now fully berserk, unsheathed his sword, drew it high over his head, and screamed. "Vengeance. Vengeance . . . now!!"

Every angel in Michael's charge began to wail and cry, even as they reluctantly drew their swords in obedience to one who was about to become disobedient.

"We must obey him who now disobeys," groaned Exalta.

"If we pass through the Door, all is lost," sobbed a grief-stricken Adorae.

# Thirteen

"A question, Michael!"

Recorder had suddenly appeared before the Door, squarely in Michael's path.

Michael's blurred eyes and dazed spirit gave testimony that he was not fully aware of who had stepped in his way.

"Who is your enemy?" roared Recorder as he drove his face into that of Michael's.

"Wha—"

"I ask, who is your enemy?"

"*He* must not harm my Lord," sputtered Michael. "I was created . . . I was created to protect the throne. When the Son became a man, my charge was to protect him. *I* am the guardian angel of no less than the Son of God. *He* . . . my enemy . . . must not be allowed to harm my Lord."

"Who is your enemy, Michael? Listen to your spirit! Find the answer. Who is your enemy?"

"My enemy. Who is my enemy? Yes, who is my enemy? He is the one who even now harms my Lord."

"Did you not hear the words of your Sovereign?

Listen to me, Michael, did you hear the words of your Lord?"

Michael's eyes brightened. "My Lord, yes. But he was struck by men. They are beating him. This cannot be allowed."

"Michael, shall you act without command? Shall you act outside your call?"

"But they must not harm my Lord," wailed a still deranged Michael.

Recorder shouted into Michael's face.

"I demand of you, Michael, as your fellow messenger, tell me who your enemy is!"

"My enemy . . . yes . . . my enemy. Who is he?" groped Michael. "He is Lucifer," trumpeted the archangel. It was the first sane word Michael had uttered since drawing his sword.

"Tell me again, Michael, who is your enemy?"

"Lucifer is my enemy," Michael repeated, flailing his sword in the air.

The angelic host began to see hope, but only because it was apparent in the face of Recorder.

"Then tell me, old comrade, shall you become as Lucifer?"

"But Recorder, they must . . . not . . . harm my Lord."

"I ask you one more time, Michael. Look into my face. Look at me, Michael! Listen to your spirit. Shall you become as Lucifer?"

"No. No," cried Michael, jerking back. "I will *never* become as Lucifer."

There were sighs, groans, tears, and soft weeping throughout the heavenly host. Michael was not yet fully sane, but he had declared with his mouth the one thing that might bring him back from the brink.

Once more Michael struggled with one overriding obsession. "But they must not harm my Lord."

"Michael. Tell me again. Shall you become as your enemy?"

"No! No!" cried Michael. "But shall I not protect my Lord? I . . . *must* protect my Lord." Michael was crying now, crying as only one does when his will has been broken.

This time Recorder's words came softly. "Did you not hear your Lord speaking? He said that darkness must have an hour to show forth its powers. Sovereignty has decreed that God's two enemies, Sin and Death, must surely have their will."

"Recorder, oh, Recorder, those two enemies of my Lord, are they not even now in alliance with *my* enemy? They will surely harm my Lord. What can be done?"

The spirit of Recorder glowed bright as he laid hold of the exact words with which to respond to Michael.

"Do you not remember?"

"Remember what?" rejoined an agitated Michael.

"That night in Egypt. Remember that awful night, Michael? Remember that wonder-filled night?"

"I remember a lamb was slain. Thousands of lambs were slain. I remember that."

"And what did he tell us?"

Michael's eyes darted about as he struggled hard to remember.

Words finally came, but they came slow and labored.

"He told us . . . he told us to come to the city of Pharaoh, to watch and learn, but to do nothing. Only to witness. We were to stand there and do nothing. We would only witness."

Sternness was in the voice of Recorder as he probed. "There was more he said to you, Michael. What was it?"

It was obvious that Michael sincerely could not remember, even as he looked about wildly, hoping to see or hear something that would remind him.

"He told me . . . what did he tell me, Recorder?"

Michael's halting words began again. "He told me . . . he told us to watch and learn because there would be . . .

"I remember, Recorder!" Michael shouted as he clutched at the robe of his ancient friend. "He told us to learn, because there would be another night. A dreadful night. A night as dreadful as was that one. And when it came, we were to do *nothing.*"

Again angels heaved grand sighs of relief.

"But, Recorder," protested Michael, "that night it was only a lamb. *This* time it is my Lord! Even as we speak he is being beaten!"

Michael's arms fell across the shoulders of Recorder. Recorder found himself holding the body of a trembling, sobbing archangel.

Michael began to wail. "O my Lord, that night has arrived. O Lord, am I to do nothing?

"Help me, Recorder!" pleaded Michael again. "My Lord is being beaten. I cannot endure such a thing."

Compassionately Recorder wrapped his arms around the mighty Michael. "Michael," Recorder's words came, gentle and almost in a whisper. *"Remember the throne."*

With those words every sinew in Michael relaxed. Michael collapsed into the arms of his companion.

"The throne. I must remember the throne," sobbed Michael.

Following those words came the sound of unnumbered millions of swords being resheathed. And with that sound came yet another: the thankful weeping of ten thousand times ten thousand angels. Gathering around their leader, the sobbing throng gradually grew still. In that moment of silence Exalta raised one hand above his head and began to sing.

*Sovereign.*
*Sovereign ever, now sovereign be.*
*Sovereign even in darksome hours.*
*Sovereign is thy throne.*
*All destiny is thine own.*
*This darkest night*
*is but light*
*to thee.*

Michael lifted his head from Recorder's cradling arms and quietly, even reverently, sheathed creation's most awesome sword.

"Fellow messengers, soon we must all return to earth. It may be that we will but relive that night in Egypt. We know nothing of what awaits us in these hours, but this we know: There is foreboding everywhere. This battle, whatever it is, is not ours to fight. Those matters lie in other hands. Soon you will return to Jerusalem just as, long ago, you went to the treasure city of Pharaoh. Yes, and as you went to Bethlehem. You will stand round about the hills of Jerusalem.

"But unless our Lord speaks, *we shall do nothing.*"

With that the angelic host slipped quietly through the Door and stepped out onto the ground around Mount Zion.

# CHAPTER
## *Fourteen*

The guards led the prisoner into the crowded streets and back toward the Antonia Fortress. Celebrators were everywhere. This night over two hundred thousand visitors crammed the streets and courtyard of the city.

From time to time the guards had to push hard against the throng in order to move toward the Roman fortress.

Farther from the temple area, the scene changed. In the western section of the city, pallets lined every street. Men, women, and children sat idly, waiting for the afternoon celebration and the evening sacrifice. Beside every Hebrew family was a little lamb.

A child watching the passing soldiers, and assuming the man with them to be a dignitary, walked up to Jesus and announced, "See my lamb. It is perfect. The priest found no fault in him." Then, seeing the chains about the Carpenter's wrists, the little boy asked innocently, "Where are they taking you?"

The response was low and whispered, "To that same place where you shall take your lamb."

As light fell upon the face of the Carpenter, the little boy stepped back in horror and, in panic, ran away.

Jesus sighed.

"Father, permit even this."

PART

II

# CHAPTER
## *Fifteen*

"Get up, Barabbas."

The prisoner opened his eyes and looked up at his intruder. "Why?" grumbled the prisoner. "It is still early. I do not die until noon. Are you trying to hurry my execution?"

"You know that you are a bit of a fool, do you not, Barabbas? There is hardly a man in all Israel who does not know your reputation, yet you tried to rob Caesar's bank to lay your hands on money for an uprising no one is interested in."

Barabbas shrugged his shoulders, then carefully turned the chains on his bruised wrists.

"Your cohorts were as much the fools as you," continued the guard.

"They were the best I could find," replied Barabbas.

"A Babylonian and an old bedouin? *That* is not much to find," laughed the soldier. "Your luck ran out a long time ago—a long, long time ago. But right now you are going to have the privilege of watching it run out one more time."

"I know," replied Barabbas.

"No, you do not," came the centurion's quick retort.

"What do you mean?" asked Barabbas cautiously as he moved toward the doorway.

"No less than Pilate has called you out this morning. He wants to see you."

"What? When has a Roman governor ever been interested in a peasant who is as good as dead?"

"It has to do with one of the customs of your Passover. A prisoner is set free on the *Day of Preparation*. Releasing a prisoner makes everyone feel good. Usually it is someone who would not be in prison more than a night or two. But not *this* year. Pilate is presenting to the people *you* and some magician from Galilee."

"I smell a rat," said Barabbas.

"Yes, and you are the rat," retorted the guard. "Pilate wants the other man set free. His wife had something to do with it. A dream of some sort. Even Herod is in on this. He could not find anything to charge the magician with, so Herod sent the man back to Pilate. To make sure it is the magician who goes free, Pilate ordered you, the most despicable, despised prisoner in Jerusalem, to be the other choice. Some choice, eh, Barabbas?"

"You are right, Roman. My luck ran out a long time ago."

"Not just yours. Your Babylonian friend and the bedouin—they die with you. At noon.

"Hear that crowd out there? The citizens of Jerusalem are about to seal your doom, Barabbas. Now get out!"

# CHAPTER
## *Sixteen*

"A murderer goes free and a harmless crank is sentenced to die," muttered a disbelieving guard.

"Which cell?"

"Throw him in the one where we kept Barabbas. It is only fitting."

"Is Barabbas really going to be set free?"

"Yes. There he comes now. But do not worry, he will be back in sight of a week."

Barabbas pushed his way past Jesus in the narrow corridor, turned, and stared at the blood-covered figure.

"What have you done to that man? Is that how you treat a magician?" queried an incredulous Barabbas.

"We almost beat him to death," replied one of the soldiers. "Thought we might get him to scream. He never did. Take a good look at him. It is what we would have done to you. Now get out of here."

Pushing Barabbas farther down the hall, the soldiers shoved the Nazarene through an open door and into the awaiting cell as he crumbled to the floor.

"What is this?" asked the officer of the two soldiers.

"It is his robe. We removed it before we beat him."

"Throw it in the cell. It belongs to him . . . until he is dead."

"Then?"

"I see you already have eyes for it. It does not matter to me. Just do not get in a fight over it."

"What have they decided about the execution?"

"He will be executed with Barabbas's two friends."

"Where?"

"On one of the hills overlooking Jerusalem. The one facing the temple. It was a request made by the high priest. Something about irony. His last sight will be the entrance to the temple. It has to do with a proverb, sir," responded the guard.

The officer turned and stared at the guard.

"What?"

"It is an ancient proverb the Jews use when anyone claims to be the Messiah. 'If he is the Messiah, let him tear the temple veil.'"

*Huh* was the officer's disinterested response.

"Will we hang them on stakes or on one of the trees?" asked another of the guards.

"Three can hang on one tree, can they not?"

"If the tree is large enough. These are such trees."

"Then the tree it will be. What about the patibula?"

"A local ironsmith made them last evening. I have them here."

"You may need only *two!* That Galilean may not live long enough to be crucified."

As the cell door slammed shut, the Carpenter, lying on the cold floor, began to whisper to someone who was in the cell with him.

"Michael?"

"My Lord. I beg you, in the name of pity, let me strike these infidels."

"No, Michael. You must not."

"Lord, I cannot continue this way. I must strike!"

"No, Michael, you will not. End such words— *now!*"

"O my Lord, my Lord!" wailed Michael.

"Hear my words, Michael. Darkness *must* have its hour. It is necessary. The cup my Father gave me awaits. Go, Michael. Find Recorder. He is expecting you. One final mission waits for you. Recorder will go with you."

"Recorder? But his place is always beside the throne. When he lays down his pen . . ."

"In a few minutes men will see me crucified here on earth. What men see will be but commonplace. Three criminals dying. But even as this happens, you and Recorder will see these same matters, only you will see them unfold as my Father sees them.

"I spare you the earthly scene, Michael. You will see these events from a grander view.

"Go, Michael. Now."

Those words spoken, the Carpenter slipped into unconsciousness. The archangel knelt beside his Lord and bade him one last tearful farewell. "Citizen of heaven, alien to earth, when shall we meet again? I depart *only* because it is your bidding."

In two hours Golgotha would become creation's center, except for two angels who were about to make an almost incredible journey . . . to places *outside* creation.

It was 10:00 A.M.

# CHAPTER
## *Seventeen*

"Quickly, Michael," urged Recorder. "This way. You and I are about to see things no eyes, save God's, have ever seen. Come. Our journey takes us where time, space, and creation have never been."

"Where then?"

"That is our first difficulty," responded Recorder, an air of consternation in his voice. "We will not be in any particular place. We will be . . ." Recorder hesitated. "What is the use of answering? Nothing I say is accurate. We will be in all places and all times."

"We are about to visit many places?"

"No, Michael." Recorder grimaced. "We will be in all places, and all time. All . . . at once."

"All places, at once?"

Recorder shook his head. "No, that is not correct, but it is as close as I can come to an explanation. Neither words, nor parables, nor revelation, nor any other means of apprehension benefit us now. We will not understand. We will only behold."

"Then you know where we are going?" responded a wholly mystified Michael.

Again frustration etched its way across Recorder's ancient brow.

"We will not go, we will surround."

"Surround?"

"We will be allowed, for one brief moment, to see as God sees." Recorder waved an arm in a gesture of futility. "That is not correct, either. It is not as God *sees,* but as God *is.* We will not so much see as he sees, but *be* where he *is.*"

Now it was Michael's turn to be frustrated.

"And *where* is that, pray tell?"

"Surrounding!"

"Surrounding what?"

"All things. Enveloping . . . all things."

"All things? What do you mean?"

"All time, all places, all eternity, all the eternals. Enveloped *in* God. Surrounded *by* God. All at once."

"How is that possible?"

"Michael, I do not know. I tell you this: He was before creation. This I know: Creation is *in* him. He surrounds and envelops creation. He surrounds and envelops all things. Not just the visible creation. Ours also. Perhaps more."

"Perhaps more than *that!* There is not more than that!"

"As I said, I do not know. Even when this journey is come to its end, I rather doubt either of us will understand. Let this be understood if understanding is possible. All things are *in* God."

Michael's eyes brightened, then dimmed. The

archangel was feeling befuddled, puzzled . . . *and* amused. And, if possible, even a little insecure.

Recorder continued.

"Before he enfolded himself into our two creations, before he made his abode inside, before that . . . he was outside. But not just outside, but surrounding creation! Even *after* coming into his creation, he still enveloped creation."

Michael looked at Recorder out of the corner of his eyes, a twinkle evident. "Then our God is far, far greater, and more mysterious, than any will ever know."

"Do not be too sure of that, Michael!"

Recorder's words could not have been more unexpected.

"What?"

"There may come a moment somewhere out there in the vast reaches of the unknown when the redeemed and the elect angels will know, even as they are known."

"Recorder, let us wisely end this conversation. Now, where do we begin our . . . ?" Michael caught himself. "An inappropriate question, I assume!"

"It may well be a very appropriate question," responded Recorder. "The answer will surprise you! Our journey *begins at the end!*"

Michael was about to register amazement when suddenly all things disappeared. Even nothingness exited the scene.

*I should lose my temper more often,* mused Michael. *Who knows what I might learn.*

At that moment something happened that is really not supposed to be possible. The two messengers were immersed in light unapproachable!

# CHAPTER
## *Eighteen*

"Where are we?"

"We are *in* that which surrounds all things."

"If I understand you, Recorder, that means we are in God! But, is that not forbidden?"

"Michael, we have always been in God. So, also, are all things. Now . . . behold!"

The immense light of glory they had been plunged into opened. Before them lay a vast panoramic scene.

Michael's eyes darted about in all directions.

"There is the *beginning* over there," cried Recorder. "And over there—there is the *end!*"

Michael's only response was to place his hands over his mouth.

"Our God is at both those places . . . at once!" exclaimed an awe-filled Recorder.

"The God we serve is at the end. At all times he is at the end. As surely as he is at the end at all times, so he is also at the beginning . . . at all times."

"He *does* envelop all things," whispered Michael, finding his voice if not his understanding.

"Michael, you have been distressed over the events taking place on earth, have you not?"

"You know I have!" responded the archangel incredulously. "Driven mad by them is more to the truth."

"And God?"

"Oh!" responded Michael, almost without breath. "He saw . . . he *sees* the final outcome, out there in the future. He sees it *now.* He is not caught as we. He *sees* the future."

"Not exactly. In fact, you could not be more mistaken," came Recorder's response. "He does *not* see the future. Nor *was* he there. He *is* in the future. He is *at* the final outcome. He *is* in today's events in Jerusalem. He is present at the finale of those events. Yet he is at the beginning, and he is at the end. All of them. *Now!* It is not that he *sees.* Rather, it simply *is.* In him."

"He knows the outcome!" exclaimed Michael.

"No!" cried an impatient Recorder. "He is at the event, he is at the outcome, right now."

Again Michael stared at Recorder as he struggled to grasp what cannot be understood.

"He is at the final outcome of today's events?" came Michael's rote answer, more to hear his words than to perceive them.

"And . . . ?" coaxed Recorder.

"Our God is *at* the *end,* right now. He is *at* the end. At all ends; at all beginnings . . . of all things. *Now.*"

"And . . . ?" continued the tutoring voice of Recorder.

"He . . . he is . . . at Golgotha." Michael swung around to face Recorder. "Now he is at the Passover in Egypt, *now.* He . . . he envelops all events. They are all in him. All at once. All creation, all times, all places are *in* him. He envelops all times!"

"More, Michael. Enveloping all things and all events, measurements of time, and all measurements of eternity, all space, the dimensionless eternals, they are always *in* him. History, ours and earth's, are surrounded by him and are in him. All things are immersed in an all-surrounding God."

"I am seeing what he is, an all-enveloping Lord presently present at the beginning and presently present at the end! Wherever I look I see that he is—not *will be*—he *is* the Omega . . . *and* the Alpha."

Recorder, having grasped all this only slightly before Michael, was struggling not to become as excited as the archangel.

"One phrase can describe it all, that is, if we could but have spirits grand enough to lay hold of its full meaning: *He is the everlasting now.*

"Michael, you are aware that I was the first living thing he ever created. I was there, at the beginning. I have always assumed all things flowed forward from that moment. But no, he created time and eternity all at once. Completed. Finished, from one end to the other.

"Unlike him, we are shackled by boundaries, travelers plodding along, part of unfolding events. And this causes us to strangely believe the future has not happened. But it has. No! It has not. But, yes, in God, it has! *We* just have not been there yet.

"He is not in the future, the future is in him.

"Things not yet, are.

"All events are in a God who envelops all."

"For one brief moment my Lord has done as he promised he would. He has allowed me to stand on some higher, broader vantage point and behold all things happening at once," responded Michael.

"Come, my friend, to the *end*. There we will behold one of the greatest Mysteries of God, how he chose the elect ones!"

"At the *end?*" questioned Michael, a corrective tone in his voice. "No, you mean at the beginning."

"No, Michael, at the *end!*"

Light broke on Michael's face as he cried in an exclamation not unlike a shout, "Our God not only foreknew us, he not only past-knew us, he future-knew us, all in the same instant!"

"Maddening, is it not?" replied Recorder in a response that could almost be called laughter. "But probably still wide of the mark. Be that as it may, you and I are about to look upon things that would dumbfound any being who is less than God."

"Even Recorder." Michael smiled, remembering he had just now *almost* seen the somber angel laugh, which was, in itself, history-making.

"Yes, Michael, even Recorder."

# CHAPTER
## *Nineteen*

"It is the redeemed. Look at them. The glorious redeemed. They are *all* gathered together in one place from all places. We are seeing that grand gathering at the end of the ages." Michael was speaking more as might a child than an archangel.

"The citizenry of salvation, the sons and daughters of God," muttered Recorder, transfixed. Then as one electrified by revelation, he cried out, "They have his Life! And his nature! They are his biological offspring, Michael. Not only adopted, but *biologically* his offspring. Sons and daughters, with God as their *biological* Father."

"They are rejoicing in the blood of the Lamb. What does that mean?" queried Michael.

"You know, Michael. You know."

"The Lamb! They are speaking of my Lord, the one who in Jerusalem is even now going to a stake. They are victorious by his blood!

"Then if he dies this day . . ." Michael hesitated. "Then that hill outside Jerusalem is not the story's end for my Lord!" Stunned by the very thought, Michael began to shake.

"So it appears," agreed Recorder, his eyes glistening with joy.

Suddenly, almost frantically, Recorder grabbed Michael.

"The Book of Life! See it. Look over there. The one our God gave to me for keeping. It is always with me, beside the throne. He gave it to me at the beginning. There it is at the *end*. Michael, do you see it?"

"Yes, I see! But, Recorder, there are no names written on its pages! The pages are *blank.*"

"That cannot be!"

There was panic in the voice of the most ancient of the angels. "I have seen every page of that book. I have seen the names of all who are marked off inside God. He marked them off in his being before creation began. So he declared it to me, and so it must be. How can the pages be blank? I tell you I have seen the names. *All* of them, recorded in that book even *before* he created. The pages cannot be blank!"

"Steady, Recorder. It was you who said we would *not* understand."

Recorder was frantic, his face pale.

"My Lord and my God, you told me the names were there *before* you dared to create. You settled their state *before.*"

From out of nowhere, yet everywhere, came a voice.

"That is not all I declared to you on that day before all days. Recorder, what else did I tell you?"

Before Recorder could even consider the answer, the Book of Life began to fill with names.

"I forgot! My Lord, forgive me. I did not realize. You were *here*—at the end—even at the instant I was there with you at the beginning. But at that selfsame moment of the beginning, you stood here at the end and watched them emerge, faithful! You knew the faithful ones here, and recorded it *there*. You saw who emerged—faithful! You saw those true to you— elect, redeemed, and faithful.

"You set them free. Free to be whatever they willed, and they chose to be yours. They followed you, and they are here at the end . . . and you are their Lord, and you are here. Yet you are also back at the beginning. I understand, though I do not understand. Lord, you saw both, all at once.

"It is here, at the *end*, you chose them! No, it was at the beginning you chose them. No, you did both, at once, in both places! No, you did it only once, but at both times. Oh, I do not know what you did. But it was on both ends that you did it!

"Of this one thing I *am* sure! Lord, within *your* being you left nothing in doubt!"

While still thrashing about in immutable revelation, Recorder suddenly threw his hands into the air.

"Look, Michael! Over there, at the very end. See! That is me over there. Michael, that is me. It is

Recorder. He . . . I . . . there at the end of all ages . . . me!

"Watch me. *Now* I understand! I have taken the Book of Life. The Book of Life, whose pages were empty, yet at the end were filled. Michael, was it I who recorded those names at the end? It is my charge to do such things. Did *I* fill in the names, at the end?"

Michael could neither move nor speak.

"Look at me! Some way, I know exactly what I am about to do! Michael, that is me, at the end, with a book that contains all the names of the redeemed. I *know* what he is—no, what I am—about to do with that book."

Recorder was verily roaring with delight, for he, though standing afar, was watching himself in the midst of the glory of the gathering of all the redeemed.

Suddenly Recorder watched himself hurl the Book of Life back through time. The Book of Life passed back through all times and ages until it came to the beginning.

Together Michael and Recorder held their breath. The Book of Life, having transversed all space and time, came to rest in the hands of God . . . at the beginning. "He who stands at the end, yet also stands in the very midst of creation as it is being born, has received the Book of Life."

Both angels stood reverently as they watched the God of the beginning call forth the recording angel out of nothing. Recorder heard again the first words the Lord ever spoke to him.

*Your name shall be Recorder.*

"That is it, Michael. That is exactly how it happened. Listen, you will hear me respond to him."

Michael's answer was gleeful. "No, Recorder, that is how it *is* happening, and how it *will* happen, and how it *did* happen."

"Watch," said Recorder, ignoring Michael's trumpeting. "Watch. He will show me one who has existed only for an instant . . . he will show me the Book of Life. I had just filled it . . . at the end, yet knew it not . . . at the beginning.

"See, I am reaching for the great, golden book. Listen to my words, spoken in utter innocence.

"My Lord, one book bears the title the Book of Life. It is already filled with names. . . ."

"Keep listening, Michael! Do you realize you are being allowed to see the very *beginning?* All this happened to me before you existed, Michael. You are seeing my genesis!"

Humbly Recorder added one more note. "At last someone is sharing with me *my birth*.

"Now, hear what our Lord said to me so long ago, and I understood it not."

*Before I created all things,*
*I finished all things.*

"Behold what Mystery. There, in the very moment of creating, when there is nothing except God, and me, he charges me with a Book I have never seen, yet *the handwriting was mine.*

"He then tells me all things are finished even before they began. He was standing at the end when he said that."

Michael turned to study the face of Recorder only to catch the ancient one doing something none would ever have imagined him to do. (Nor did Michael ever relate to anyone the events of that moment.) Recorder, quite beside himself, began shouting, crying, flailing his arms about, and generally conducting himself more like Exalta than the ever-reserved angel of the records.

"Old friend," whispered Michael, tears flowing down his cheeks as he watched the unsightly conduct of his venerable friend, "I only hope that when our Lord allows you to return to time, and to the eternals, he will allow you the memory of this moment."

Recorder turned a tearstained face toward Michael. "He is beyond all knowing. He is sovereign. Oh, is our God sovereign," cried Recorder, weeping. "He said to me that he finished all things *before* he created all things. You know what else he told me? And I still do not fully understand. He told me that he had been slain *before* the foundations of creation."

Recorder drew in a deep breath, then continued.

"Michael, we must go. I have seen the unbelievable. Now, I perceive it is time for *you* to see the unbelievable. We are about to see things that concern you. Perhaps we may even be allowed to glimpse an event that happened *after* the end."

Once again the two messengers were swallowed up in light.

# CHAPTER
## *Twenty*

"Recorder, I cannot see you. I sense you are beside me. Take my hand."

"Do you know what it is we are about to see?" responded the recording angel.

"Of course not, but some things are clear to me. He will die today at Jerusalem. I . . . I shall not be able to prevent it."

"And?"

"The chosen ones, the redeemed. They are in him. Therefore, should he die, they will die with him."

"Is that all?"

"Surely not! Somewhere out there he will triumph. I can only believe that someday he will live again. There is obviously final triumph out there somewhere."

"If so?"

"If he lives again, they will also live again, for they are in him."

Once more the light opened before them.

# CHAPTER
## Twenty-One

"There, Michael . . . near the end. See?"

"It is Lucifer," snarled Michael. "He is still seeking to win a battle he will lose."

"Still seeking to win a battle he *has lost!*" whispered Recorder.

"Look, something else there at the end. Death! Oh, Death is dead!"

To their surprise, the scene suddenly changed.

"Jerusalem! We are seeing what is happening in Jerusalem at this very moment, as earth knows time."

"It is my Lord hanging on a loathsome tree." Michael found himself once more slipping into rage.

"Steady, Michael. Dare to keep looking. Be of courage."

"My Lord is dying. Yet I have this comfort: His enemy, Death, is also dying. Thank God, Death is dying. But, oh, at what price."

"What else, Michael? Watch closely. What else is he taking with him in the grave?"

"I see nothing."

"A moment ago our God allowed me to see myself at the end of creation. You are about to see yourself *at* Golgotha! Steady, old friend. Do not move. Only behold."

"There I am! The Lord is giving me powers over space and time."

The two angels continued to stare at a scene not yet born, yet there was the archangel taking wings across history, transversing all matter, time, and the spiritual.

"See, Michael. It is you. At the end!"

"Look!" shouted Michael. "I am come to my archenemy, Lucifer. Ah! This is the battle for which I live. Behold, Recorder, see me! I am at last drawing my sword on that archdemon."

"You are driving Lucifer back through history, forcing *him* back across time."

"Look! Recorder, it is to Golgotha I have forced him. I am driving my enemy back . . . to the cross. The Lord has driven his enemy—Death—into the grave with him. Now he shall allow me to drive my enemy into the same destructive grave along with Death. Shall I force that fiend back to where Death and Life are dying?"

Like a spectator witnessing combatants in some grand arena, Recorder began to cheer. "Drive him back! Drive him to the cursed tree! Drive him, Michael, to his destruction.

"Drive him to the destroying tree!

"Lucifer! See his face. He is amazed. He did not know! He, too, was dealt with at Golgotha. My enemy, I drive you into the bosom of the Son of God. Lord, destroy him upon the tree."

As though seeing through a distant portal, the two angels witnessed Death, Sin, and Lucifer sink into the bosom of the Crucified One.

"From that hour, on Golgotha's hill, the Prince of Darkness was the ever-defeated foe, yet knew it not!

"We have learned of a God, and of a Lamb slain before the foundation of the world. Yet all the while he also stood at the end. Lucifer was defeated *before* creation. By a slain Lamb."

Once again, the scene changed.

The two angels fell silent. They had become intruding witnesses to the final moments of creation.

Michael clutched at Recorder's arm. "The finale. I deal the final blow to my cursed enemy."

"It would be wiser if you would turn and look at what I am seeing, Michael. The whole panorama of creation is here. But this time we truly see as God sees. *Look at Golgotha.*"

With great reluctance Michael turned away from the victorious scene he was witnessing.

Michael gasped.

What the two angels saw could not be communicated, not by the tongue of men or angels.

Future and past had relinquished their titles! Creation no longer moved forward in a straight line, but had swung about into a vast circle. At the very center of that grand circling stood the cross. All things that were in time and eternity now moved around their true center . . . the Christ of the cross.

"There is something else there, beside the cross."

# CHAPTER
## Twenty-Two

"What is that which lies so near the cross?"

"A tomb, I believe."

"Michael, we see the crucifixion as God sees it. No! We see Golgotha and the tomb as they *really* are. All creation finds its center in them."

Awestruck, the two messengers watched as all points of a circular creation began flowing toward the cross.

"All creation is being brought back to its center!" whispered Recorder. "The cross is drawing all things into its destroying vortex."

"What is this the cross is doing?" stammered Michael.

"Has done, Michael. Has already done. It is destroying the entire creation!"

Michael shook his head. "Shall I ever learn that which I see? Everything is moving toward the cross. All things in creation, and creation itself, are coming to an end. *Have* come to an end!"

"And more."

"I see things being destroyed by the cross that shall

bring great joy, not only to elect angels, but also to the redeemed.

"All those rules no one can keep, or even understand. They are destroyed in the cross. Those ordinances no one could live up to, annihilated by the cross. All those commandments that no one ever discovered how to obey! Now vanished."

". . . and the Sabbath," added Recorder.

". . . and all the special days people tried to observe perfectly, but *never* did," continued Michael.

"We are watching the entire fallen creation, all things *not* redeemed, slip to utter destruction.

"Thank God," breathed Recorder. "The end of the fall. The end of all evidence of the fall."

"Look—some monstrous cloud! For a moment it appeared over Jerusalem but just as suddenly vanished. It slipped into the being of the Son of Man."

"Sin," instructed Recorder. "The annihilation of Sin."

The entire creation act inexorably slipped into the eternal cross.

"Creation, crucified!" murmured Recorder.

"Even the elect . . . chosen at the beginning (*and* the end) drawn into the cross . . . and into him," intoned Michael.

"It is only proper," replied Recorder. "Plunged into his death. Immersed in him even in his death, therefore dying with him. See them. All of them. Flowing into death with him. They were in him *before* creation. They are in him at the end. They are always in him!"

Recorder, considering his words, raised his arms high above his head in an act of profoundest praise.

"They are in you, regardless of the age or ages. Wherever they are to be found in that long trek from alpha to omega, each and all are always *in* you.

"They die in you. They are dead to all that died in you. Dead to sin. Dead to that miserable, fallen creation that we even now see being drawn to its final hour. Six days to create. Only a moment and a cross to destroy. And, if you live again, so shall they.

"Men are watching a very ordinary execution in Jerusalem. We are beholding the same event, in God, and we witness the crucifixion of creation.

"Our time here is over, Michael. We must go."

"Where are the sands of time, Recorder?"

"When we return, I believe our Lord will be breathing his last, or perhaps he is already dead. Perhaps even entombed."

"Will he live again, Recorder?"

"I know not all things, but this I know. The marked-off ones are in him. Alive or dead, past or future, they are in him.

"I know a little about my Creator. He wove his most treasured secrets into the fabric of creation, there to be seen if we have eyes to see.

"I have seen a seed planted in the ground. It dies, as well you know. Yet I have seen that same seed rise out of the earth. *It was my Lord who created seed.*

"Further, that seed is not alone as it rises. It has become many seeds. Whatever time or age it will be, of this I am certain: He will live again, and the redeemed will also live again."

Once more the light of the being of God enveloped the two angels.

"We will be allowed one more scene," observed Recorder. "It will be brief."

Again the light parted.

"Where are we, and what is that?"

# CHAPTER
# *Twenty-Three*

All things had vanished, except a tomb.

"Where is everything, Recorder?"

"I believe we will discover that all else exists *not*. *There is only a tomb.* All things in creation and creation itself are locked in that tomb. All! Forever!"

Michael reached out to touch the tomb.

Recorder stayed his hand.

"There are only two things for an archangel to fear. One is an instrument of death so great it could destroy even creation. The other is a tomb so glorious that it could give birth to a new creation."

"A new creation!" stammered Michael. "Yes, of course, with the fallen creation gone, he is free to create again.

"If he rises—no, if he is already risen—his chosen are also risen. If he rises, if he is risen, they *are* alive and risen, and dead to the old creation. Dead to sin, dead to the whole fallen universe. Alive to him, and alive in a new creation.

"No . . . alive *as* a new creation.

"Perhaps it is my imagination, but it seems the tomb has begun to tremble," observed Michael.

Recorder was about to reply when the two old travelers were again enveloped in light. "You were right, Recorder, a *very* brief moment here."

There was flash; then for an instant an opening to another scene, but so quickly did it vanish that neither messenger could know for certain what he saw.

"A scene beyond the end?" asked Recorder. "Did I see all the elect gathered? Then, flowing back into him . . . from whence they came.

"I am certain I saw a girl. The girl. His bride. Becoming one. One with him. Then dissolving into him," muttered Recorder.

Then adding a question even as he disappeared again into an ocean of light and glory, "He who was once the All, becoming the All in All?"

PART

IV

# CHAPTER
## *Twenty-Four*

The East Gate swung open. In the distance was the road to Bethany, beside the road the highest of the hills overlooking Jerusalem. A giant tree, its wood bleached, its trunk hard as stone, rose from the pinnacle of the hill.

A squad of four soldiers pushed their prisoner out into the morning light.

"Hand him the crossbeam. Put it on his shoulders. The prisoner must carry his own instrument of death as a lesson to onlookers.

"Prisoner, take the crossbeam! Do you understand?"

"Yes," replied the Carpenter. "I have understood the ways of the cross for a long, long time."

With those words the Carpenter reached out and took the crossbeam, balanced it on one shoulder, and stepped out onto the road to Bethany.

"We will never get through this melee," grumbled one of the soldiers. "Everyone in Israel is pushing toward the temple. We are the only ones going outside the gate."

"Push the crowd aside. Use the whip if necessary."

"Hold. Here come the other two squads with their prisoners, and Abenadar on horseback. This may not take so long after all. Let us just hope we can get this prisoner up that hill before he dies."

Jesus raised his head. The open fields between Bethany and Jerusalem were a mass of humanity moving as one toward the temple. The entire landscape glistened like snow.

"As far as I can see, the lambs. They have caused everything to look pure white."

The bleating of the little ewes blended together to create a strange, unearthly hymn.

"From the crest of the hill I will be able to look down and see it all. Passover is about to begin. The citizens of Jerusalem will watch as man and lamb die together.

"Father, permit even this."

At that moment the other two squads joined the first. Twelve soldiers and their prisoners pushed out onto the road, Abenadar leading the way with horse and whip.

Caught in the push and pull of the melee, the Carpenter was repeatedly knocked to the ground. Each time, the soldiers pulled him to his feet. But on the final occasion he not only collapsed, his body began shaking violently.

"He is down. He cannot bear that crossbeam alone. Revive him, and find someone to carry the cross," commanded Abenadar.

"You there, slave. Yes, you! Take this man's cross-beam, African."

"It does not serve one well to stand out in a crowd," muttered Simon as he reached down and grasped the beam of wood.

Jesus struggled to his feet, but just as quickly collapsed again. The Cyrenean knelt down and took the prisoner in his arms.

"Simon of Cyrene?"

"You know me?"

"I have always known you."

"No," protested Simon, "I do not know *you.*"

"Do you not have two sons? One, Alexander, the other, Rufus."

"You *do* know me! Where have we met?"

"All right, prisoner, up on your feet," ordered a guard.

Simon looked into the face of the soldier, then at Jesus, then lifted the Carpenter to his feet.

"Carry his burden. All the way up the hill."

"Where, man, have we met?"

"Simon, follow me."

"To the hill?"

"Forever!" replied the Carpenter.

Effortlessly Simon swung the crosspiece over his shoulder.

*Simon,*
*beyond this day*
*thy guest*

*shall I be,*
*not in thy home*
*but in thee.*

A band of soldiers, three criminals, and a slave from Cyrene slowly made their way toward a high hill overlooking Jerusalem, the temple, and the courtyard surrounding the temple. The whole scene was now white with innocent lambs, all about to be slaughtered for the atoning of the sins of mankind.

# CHAPTER
## Twenty-Five

Three crossbeams dropped to the earth. The Carpenter crumbled to the ground with them.

The soldiers, as trained, drew their swords and formed a semicircle around the prisoners, signaling to all that no interference with the ensuing proceedings would be tolerated.

Jesus again staggered to his feet. He turned again to look down upon that city which so often slew its prophets. Just beyond the east wall he saw the temple.

"The doors to the temple. Beyond, the veil, and beyond the veil, the Holy of Holies. The last sight I shall behold; then another Door, in another realm."

The Carpenter turned slightly to his left. Only a few yards away, on the side of the same hill he stood upon, lay the altar of the scapegoat.

"As the scapegoat, so am I, *outside the camp.* Father, permit even this."

"That is not Barabbas," shouted the thief known simply as the bedouin. "What happened to Barabbas?"

Hearing the bedouin's words, the Babylonian turned to look at the unknown criminal. "Who is this? I cannot see his face for the blood. I am particular with whom I die."

Several of the Roman guards laughed at the macabre humor.

"Whoever he is, his own mother would not recognize him," responded the bedouin almost softly.

"Barabbas has been released," intruded one of the soldiers. "This one is far worse the criminal. Barabbas only stole and murdered. This one frightened the city fathers. No man should ever be so much the fool."

"Who is he?" repeated the bedouin.

"He is your companion in death. That is all you need to know," replied one of the soldiers.

"Who is he?" demanded the bedouin.

This time it was Abenadar who answered.

"Last week he was a hero. The whole city turned out to greet him right here on the Bethany road. Palm branches, singing, everything. This week he is the enemy of the state and of Rome."

"What did he do?" asked the Babylonian, intent on keeping his mind off the impending proceedings.

"Something about claiming to be the Son of God," replied the soldier standing nearest the bedouin. "Now turn around, both of you. I will untie your hands, but remember, a sword is at your neck."

A moment later the dreaded words were spoken.

"Lie down on your crossbeam. Stretch out your arms. Mind my words or take the whip."

Three soldiers grabbed the bedouin and dragged him to the crosstimber, forcing him to the ground and spreading his arms out onto the patibulum.

As he felt cold iron press to his wrist, the bedouin began protesting and kicking. There was a dull thud. The bedouin screamed. The hammer had found its mark.

He screamed again, this time adding curses on God and man.

"Shut up, bedouin!" yelled one of the guards as he slapped the Bedouin's other arm hard against the crossbeam. "Be content that you are dying with God!"

# CHAPTER
## *Twenty-Six*

"Haul the Jew up first, or he may not live long enough to be crucified. It will take two ladders; get them over here, now."

"I must face the temple."

"Did he say something?"

"He asked to be nailed on the west side of the tree, facing the temple."

Four soldiers, two on each side, seized the patibulum upon which Jesus' arms had been nailed. The soldiers, expecting the usual screams, noted their victim groan only quietly as he was hoisted off the ground and onto the tree.

"A king so meek. No wonder they feared him."

The patibulum was quickly nailed to the tree. For a moment the feet of the Carpenter dangled loosely, his full weight pulling at his pierced wrists. But only for a moment. One of the soldiers seized his feet, placed them one on the other, and pushed them upward. In the next instant a long spike found its way through his feet. The soldiers were about to dismount the ladders when Abenadar spoke.

"We are not finished. Take this piece of wood Pilate scrawled on. Nail it to the tree, above the crossbeam. Let all the world see this man's crime."

"Such an unmentionable crime," said the soldier as he nailed the sign to the tree.

*JESUS OF NAZARETH*
*KING OF THE JEWS*

Next the Babylonian was nailed to the tree, facing north, then the bedouin, facing south, both hanging slightly lower than the Carpenter.

The screams and cries of the two thieves blistered the air. Pilgrims in the temple courtyard, hearing the wails, looked up to identify the commotion. The far-off laments of the two thieves blended with the bleatings of the thousands of lambs in the courtyard.

Eventually the cries of the two thieves became intermittent. The loudest noise being heard on Golgotha's hill was now the jeers of religious men who had climbed the hill to ridicule the Carpenter.

It was high noon.

The paschal lamb would die in six hours.

# CHAPTER
## *Twenty-Seven*

"You must not go, Mary."

The voice belonged to John. "That kind of dying is the most hideous of things."

"I was his passageway out of his world into mine. I watched him come into our realm from places we know not. I will not be held back from seeing him pass out of this foreign world back into that celestial abode from which he came."

John's protestations ended. Mary had that way about her, a certain finality that came with her words. A young carpenter named Joseph had heard her speak that way and yielded. Even her son, at a wedding in Cana, had known her firm and persistent ways. And today Mary spoke thus to a young disciple who would, before nightfall, take her as his adopted mother.

"If it must be, then I shall be your guide to that terrible place," replied an acquiescent John.

"We will go too." The voice was that of Mary Magdalene. Salome, wife of Zebedee, and Joanna nodded in assent.

"He must see that I am there," added Mary Magdalene.

*It is no wonder we often called you the Magdalene—the fortress,* thought John.

Sighing, John spoke aloud. "This will be the worst day you will ever live. Mary, you are not prepared for this. No mother could be."

"But I am," came her soft reply. "Long ago a very imposing messenger from the other realm told me of his birth. And the Spirit told me of his death, that it would be as a dagger to my heart. For thirty-four years I have prepared myself for this hour."

"But, Mary, it is Golgotha."

"I know."

"It is by crucifixion."

"This I also know."

"By sundown, Mary, your son will be no more."

Mary's eyes darted toward John's face.

"Do not be too certain of that, John."

# CHAPTER
## Twenty-Eight

"Did he really say he was God?" inquired the Babylonian, speaking through clenched teeth.

Without looking, one of the soldiers playing knucklebones near the base of the tree replied, "The *Son* of God."

The Babylonian twisted his head around toward the west. "If you *are* the Son of God," he railed, "then surely a few Roman soldiers will not deter you from escape. Come down off this tree, and bring me with you. I swear to you, Son of God, if you bring me down, I will change my ways. I will stop being a thief. I will become a beggar." The Babylonian laughed at his own wit.

There was a moment's silence, then the Babylonian began again. "Is God stopped by a handful of nails?" Again he laughed at his own enigmatic jeer.

The bedouin joined in the mocking. "Come down from this tree and save me. This is not the way I wish to die. If you are the Son of God, now is the time to prove it."

The bedouin moaned and fell silent. His tauntings had extricated a heavy toll on his body.

One of the priests standing before Jesus finished his words for him. "Yes, if you are the Son of God, come down. I will believe in you. I will bow to you. Even follow you."

To this mockery the Living Sacrifice responded not a word.

The day passed into afternoon, while nails, heat, and fever took their toll on the spasming bodies of the trees' three victims. As the hours passed, each man found it more difficult to marshal the strength to push and pull himself up on nothing more than nails driven through his feet and hands, balance, breathe, and then collapse, exchanging excruciating pain in the feet for unbearable pain in the arms, wrists, and hands. For all three men the end of living on a planet called earth was coming to a close.

Buzzards circling above waited patiently for prey. Not so the insects. Almost from the outset they had swarmed about the three dying men, adding yet one more agony to endure in their inexorable trek toward death.

Late afternoon, as time grew dull for the guards, one of them looked up at the bedouin, who was struggling hardest to breathe, and asked, "Bedouin, how does it feel to die with God?"

The bedouin grimaced and turned his head away. But then, from deep within his bosom, a question formed. "Where have I heard that phrase before? . . . Long ago someone uttered a similar word to me."

At that moment the Babylonian rekindled his derisive comments toward the Carpenter.

"If you are the Son of God . . . you have only a few moments left to prove it. Pull yourself free of the beam and this tree. . . . Step down upon the earth . . . then come and free me. . . . I will even follow you. . . . Like Barabbas, I will pick up a sword . . . and slay your Roman executors."

For reasons inexplicable the other thief shot back. "Shut up, Babylonian. . . . Barabbas murdered a Roman. . . . You and I are guilty of our crimes. . . . We die justly. Leave the Carpenter alone. . . . Let him die in his solitude. . . . He has done nothing wrong."

Again the thief tried hard to remember some long-forgotten conversation he had had back in his youth. *Someone once said to me, "If God came to earth, if he would live here and learn what it was to be hungry, if he saw all the disease and pain, the weakness, if he came out of heaven and became a man, saw the poverty and disease . . . if he were to come here and discover just how easy it is for men to sin and how difficult it is not to."*

*Who said this to me?* wondered the now-dying thief.

*A rabbi . . . out in the desert. Was it he who spoke those words to me . . . long ago? We were out in the desert. In a caravan. What did that old rabbi say to me?*

*Would you believe in God if he came to earth, learned the injustices that men are capable of, even tasted those* injustices, just as you have? If he were to learn just how unfair men can be to other men. What if he came and died as you will die, alone and forsaken?*

Astonishment raced across the bedouin's face.

*Those words. No. The old rabbi did not speak those words to me. It was I who spoke those words to him! "If God would come to earth and die as I will die, alone and forsaken. If he would do that, then would I believe."*

*Those were my words. I spoke those words!*

Turning his head, the thief became aware of Jesus in a new way. "Let him die with me . . . alone, forsaken . . . unjustly."

The Lord turned his face toward the thief. "Did you know that you cannot seek him except you have already found him?"

"It is him! He really did come down here!"

On that day when all Jesus' followers had forsaken him, there was but one man in all the world who called him *Lord*. It was an old bedouin.

"Lord!" cried the bedouin. "O Lord, when you come into your kingdom, *remember me!*"

Out from the inmost being of the Carpenter came the voice of One who had dwelt within him since he had been conceived in the womb of Mary. That voice would respond to the thief's simple request.

*Bedouin,*
*I have known you and loved you*
*from before the foundation of this world.*
*This day shall you be with me in paradise.*

There was a long silence, then in a tone quite foreign even to the bedouin, the thief gave his quiet response.

"Lord, when I arrive there, please place me in the nurseries of heaven."

The Lord raised his head and smiled.

*Bedouin,*
*close your eyes;*
*end your pain.*
*Then open them again.*
*Look all about and see*
*the glory you have gained.*
*Die now*
*that we may meet again.*

Jesus spoke again, but this time he spoke to a dark creation in realms unseen.

"The hour of darkness has arrived. I call forth my servant, Death. Hear my voice, you who dwell within the netherworld. It is your time. Come, incarnate Death. Come, Azell. Come now to Golgotha."

Suddenly time stood still. Creation vanished. There now existed nothing but a cross and a dying Carpenter. But in the dark distance could be heard the gurgling voice of Death as he moved toward the Carpenter.

PART

V

# CHAPTER
## *Twenty-Nine*

Deep in the caverns of the netherworld, seen only by eyes long since closed, there rose a dark, seraphic form.

"I hear you, Nazarene!" howled Azell. "At last, my highest hour—and your last! Now must all things die. Except me! I, Azell, who ne'er have been alive, forever dead, alone shall live."

Standing in the center of the labyrinths of the netherworld, Azell bellowed a soliloquy to his greatness.

> *I alone*
> *am worthy to be the god*
> *of this wretched creation.*
> *I cancel puny man's pathetic reality.*
> *Show forth this truth,*
> *that truth is found*
> *only in grim fatality.*
>
> *I am justice*
> *for all who go unpunished*

*for their ill-gotten gain.*
*They find retribution only in me,*
*for by my breath*
*they are slain.*
*All other lords but speak in vain*
*when they pronounce that*
*tomorrow bears no pain.*

*I am man's true liberty.*
*I am the peace he so long has sought.*
*I am man's final search.*
*I am his highest ascent.*
*I am the final good.*
*Beyond me there is but nought.*

*It is I alone who give man eternal oneness,*
*For I make him one with nothingness.*

*I am powerful beyond the greatest sovereign.*
*Hear me, all*
*who have in space and time or eternity*
*been begotten.*
*When I rule, even God shall be forgotten.*

*I am the best of hope,*
*the end of fear,*
*the banisher of all pretense.*
*When I reign,*
*of sin, of man, of gods or God*
*shall be no whit of evidence.*

*I end all disputes,*
*annihilate all covenants.*
*I drink the heavens, earth, and sea.*
*States, rules, kingdoms, and kings*
*bequeath their all to me.*
*The great, the small are equal in my presence.*
*Be they creatures, men, or gods,*
*enter they must into my portal.*
*In my presence all are mortal.*

*Always I arrive too early.*
*Man bolts his door to ward me off*
*and breathes a prayer he will not be found.*
*Yet every door leads to me*
*and every key is mine.*
*In my domain no door nor key*
*can all his seeking find.*

*Though I be god of all,*
*reserved for me is creation's greatest contempt.*
*To my altar none ascend.*
*I am worshiped by none.*
*From this draw I my full content.*

*The cradle sits beside the grave.*
*All things live*
*within the shadow of my habitat.*

*You who fear me most have least*
*for which to live.*

*To you I come with grandest glee*
*and laugh at your vain attempt*
*to flee.*

*I am the passageway for all*
*into the blank.*
*Unlike my prey,*
*I have never lived.*
*I ascend above the highest immortality.*

*Man, my forfeit, my tribute,*
*slip into my coffer upon demand.*
*I slay you all,*
*even if you were born*
*before the fall.*

*When I come for you,*
*your deepest fear nor highest prayer*
*nor grandest gift*
*can cause another your place to take.*
*If you for only one day did breathe,*
*you will find me in your wake.*

*Oh, vast heaven, in your beauty—*
*earth, you bright blue ball—*
*come to your funeral*
*I so well have planned.*
*There shall all memory of you die*
*by my contemptuous hand.*

*Only one hope*
*ever have you had*
*against my call.*
*And he now hangs dying*
*upon a high mound*
*that is bloody and bald.*

*Weak God, hanging upon a lifeless tree,*
*in pathos does he beckon me.*
*He, my only enemy—*
*hear him call?*
*He invites me to come to him.*
*For even he*
*longs to be*
*one with Death's grand fraternity.*

*Foolish God, born of woman's womb—*
*no hand, not even yours,*
*can keep you from your tomb.*
*I come, O Nazarene,*
*to hear your lips confess.*
*My place is high above you.*
*Today I shall see*
*creation's God bow to me.*
*In return my highest gift*
*shall I give to you—*
*even Death's immortality.*

"Carpenter, you who fashioned tables, chairs, and creation, I rise to the surface one final time to claim my last victory. Even *you!*"

With these words the region of the dead opened its staircase to the surface of the earth.

# CHAPTER
## *Thirty*

The bowels of the netherworld exploded. Death emerged before the cross.

In obedience to the Carpenter, time and eternity had ceased their turn. Earth, sky, and heaven had taken their leave. The only thing remaining was a stage of nothingness, and upon it nought but a dying man, a cross, and Death.

"All hours are yours, save one, Nazarene," announced the angel of death, who also bore the name Azell. "That one hour belongs to me. Yet shall that hour last forever. Today shall it be found that Death is greater than Life. Your eternity will seem brief when compared to the everlasting grave I have prepared for you."

When Death's vaunted railings ceased, the Carpenter replied, "If you are so great, O Death, why have you not already slain me?"

Death winced but did not reply.

"Why, there in Egypt," continued the Carpenter, "why did you not pass beyond my blood? When Lucifer came to me in the desert, why did you not kill me? Why so long this wait? Even now I invite you to take me!"

"I will slay you this hour. When finished here, I alone will be called god," threatened Azell.

"Then kill me now, Azell!"

There followed only silence.

"You do not, because you cannot!"

"I will!" protested Death.

"Then do so now. I defy you."

Again Death neither answered nor moved.

"Tell me, Death, how came you to be in my creation?"

Death's eyes glistened, his lips smacked in remembrance of that day.

"I came into your creation by means of the one who begat me! That one sent me into your trite creation," answered Death proudly.

"You speak the truth, pale Azell. You came into my creation by means of Sin. Since all men have sinned, therefore, all are your prey. Yet, you cannot come to me unless *I* oblige you."

Bloodlust seeped through every word as Death yelped, "Yes, yes. All sin, therefore, all are mine!"

"Yes, Azell. All . . . but *one!* You cannot take me, for I have not sinned. Hear me, Death, I am outside your jurisdiction."

At that declaration Death whimpered, then burst into fury. "You will be mine. Today. I *know* it!"

"You have come to claim, not only me, but both of my creations, have you not? Then will you carry all I have created into the grave. In your hands creation will become vapor."

"Less than vapor!" crowed Death.

"Azell, be reminded that creation dropped from my finger long before you arrived. Before that, much happened of which you know nothing!

"I had Purpose in creation. I do not mean to be deterred. In that primordial age, creation was perfect, though there was one who remained incomplete. Man! My Purpose for him was that he become one with me. Shall you prevent me from this?"

"Ah! But, Carpenter, man chose not that oneness with you. And in his disobedience something dark came into your creation. It was me, yes, it was me!" exclaimed Death. "I came. I, Azell, the angel of death."

"No, Azell. Not you. Something even *before* you?"

Death's eyes darted with sinister excitement. "Ah! That is the best part, Carpenter.

"Sin came first, *then* did Sin beget *me*. I was birthed by Sin! Oh, marvelous fate. I, who am about to be god of all things, came into your creation by wondrous, monstrous, hideous *Sin*. Out of the bowels of the *non* I arose. Though alive, yet dead. Though dead, yet alive! Yes, Sin came into your creation, Carpenter. Sin dragged your creation from glory to filth. *Then* came Sin's masterpiece. I, Death, am that masterpiece!"

Frothing wildly, Death raised his hands above his

head and roared as might ten thousand demons crying at once.

"Yes! I came into the world, and your worthless Purpose will never be realized. The title deed to creation passes to me. *Today.* As surely as you created it and Sin cursed it, so shall I obliterate it."

Death paused, his eyes flashing fire. "Ah, but you must know this, dying Carpenter. All that we speak of is insignificant to me. Herein is my greater joy. I shall destroy *you!* Creation shall be my toy, yes. To crush into nothingness, yes. But the heart of my heart is to make you *mine.* My proudest delight is *you!"*

"You will destroy me, Death? You cannot." The Lord's next words came slow and deliberate. "You enter only where there is *Sin.* Where there is not Sin, you cannot enter."

The Lord scowled at Death. "Where Sin ceases, so, also, do all your boasted powers."

Death's glee vanished as dreadful reality pierced him.

"Do you not know why I have invited you here, Death? A unique man allowed Sin into this creation. Your words are true. Sin now reigns here. You reign also, but only because of the reign of Sin. But then came I into this world, a man as unique as that first man. You came into existence by his disobedience. It may be that *you* will be vanquished, today, by the obedience of the second man."

"You think to save your fallen creation, Carpenter?" sneered Death. "You cannot. We are locked. It is true that I cannot put you to death except by Sin, but always remember your creation is damned and is held fast in the hands of Sin and Death."

"I have called you here today because I intend to pay that unpayable price to redeem creation and fallen man."

The hands of Death shot above his head.

"Ah, day of wonders! At last you speak sanity, Carpenter. We twin monsters, Sin and Death, who have slipped as aliens into your realm, we alone are the means for you to gain back this gored creation."

"What is your demand, O Death?"

Death could hardly hide his perverse joy as he considered the scene: Life and Death negotiating for creation.

Death swept his hand out before the Son of God.

"Look! Look carefully. See my kingdom?

"Note that all which are within it are still. Behold! All lie in endless sleep. Not one will ever live nor leave. They sinned! In that moment they each became mine! I have kidnapped them. One and all."

"To relinquish them, what ransom do you demand?"

"Yes. Oh yes. What *is* my ransom?" replied the jocular fiend. "This. Come and *work* for *Sin!* It need be only a moment. Carpenter, come be found in Sin's employment. For your labors, a wage will be paid you."

"What will Sin pay me, if I should work for Sin, if—as you say—it be 'only for a moment'?"

"I . . . oh, murderous thought . . . *I* am the wage that Sin will pay you. Work for Sin, receive *me* as your wage, then will I release *half* my prey from my dark domain."

"I have a better offer, Azell." But the Lord's words came far more as a command than as bargaining.

"Bring all sin here. *All* sin. I will do more than serve as Sin's employee. I shall become *one* with Sin. For this ransom, when paid, you will release *all*. You, Death, must relinquish all your booty!"

Death squirmed with delight.

"You, who are purity, will become impurity? You will become Sin? Sin itself? You will do this in order to release mankind from Sin and from *me!* What better bargain can there be! I trade you this fallen cesspool of humanity, and in return I capture *you . . . forever!*

"You shall die, Carpenter! In dying go to your grave believing you shall destroy my progenitor. Die believing you shall destroy me. But once I hold you to my breast, once my claws steal your last breath, you shall stir no more. Forever! Then, dead, you cannot prevent me. Then am I the final god!" howled Azell.

"Your purpose: to destroy creation and Creator," responded Jesus. "My Purpose: to become one with those whom I chose before creation."

The Carpenter drew in a deep breath, then began to speak those words that Death had craved to hear from the moment he first entered the realm of things alive. It was of no consequence that the Carpenter hurled them to him as a defiant challenge.

"Death, you are free to call forth Sin . . . free to call Sin to this place."

The very thought sent Death into ecstasy. Thrusting forth his chest, he shrieked,

*Sin my knife,*
*God my victim,*
*creation my booty.*
*Annihilation my joy!*

"Bring here, to me, the monster of all monsters. But I warn you, Azell, many of those who have tasted Sin will, by the obedience of a man, be made right in the eyes of God.

"Finally, Azell, you must know your risk. When I created, I vowed to myself that on the sixth day I would cease all creating acts. If this creation dissolves, then am I free of that vow. Then am I free to create anew, to bring forth a *new creation.*"

Azell began to laugh hysterically.

"Can a dead God create? That which is dead cannot live, much less can he create. Such jest in the face of your demise is admirable but impotent!"

"You have been warned, Azell. Now do your worst."

Death turned away from the cross and began screeching the most abominable of all incantations.

123

# CHAPTER
## *Thirty-One*

Hands flailing the air, Death began to sing his mad song.

"Come, my mother! Come, you who bore me out of your filthy womb.

> *Come from the east,*
> *all deeds of demons.*
> *Come from the west,*
> *all wickedness of witchcraft.*
> *Come from the north,*
> *all sorcery and sacrilege.*
> *Come from the south,*
> *all diabolic depravity.*
> *Come to the skull.*
> *Make thyself one*
> *with God's only Son.*

"Come all impurity, come all wantonness. Come, all that is perverse. Come corruption. Come unchastity. All that is unpardonable and unforgivable . . . make haste to me. All that is loathsome, rotten, and decadent, come. Great perversity and prodigality, come.

"From all places and all time, come. Gather yourself into one, to this place where innumerable lambs have been slain. Come to Moriah, where Isaac should have been mine. Come, my mother, bring your grotesque self here to me, your loyal son. Together we shall feast upon our only enemy, our last victim, our final prey. He is ours to devour!

*Invidia*

*Avaritia*

*Acedia*

*Vitiare*

"Forsake all others of your prey. There is but one upon whom to fall. All that is not righteous, all that is not holy, all that is not God, bring here. Come! Make the Carpenter your full possession. Nay! *Make him to be yourself!*"

Death's perverse incantation ended.

Out from the graves of all mankind it came. From out of the sea, from the frozen north, from the deserts of the earth. From every tick of time and every inch of creation came the accumulation of all the sickness of Sin, gathering itself into one great fomentation of abomination.

On and on came vile clouds of stench and gore, wallowing their way toward the cross and the Carpenter.

At last the totality of the excrement of Sin gathered as one maddened whirlwind, dancing about Golgotha.

Evil was all.

"You have heard my hideous incantation. You have come, my mother. Freed from the captivity of time you have dragged yourself here, O bloated filth!

> *Thy task is one.*
> *Annihilate that beast called Life,*
> *who permissioned thee here.*
> *Take this king who knows not*
> *that he can die.*
> *Then crown me with his fallen diadem.*
> *Make me the final god.*

Gradually the monstrousness of the monstrosity of Sin shaped itself into its final form. Even Death, sickened by the sight of incarnate gore, doubled over with nausea.

"All is here. Do you attend to my words, Creator and Carpenter? All Sin is *here,*" screeched Death.

The eyes of Death flashed flames of black and yellow as, intoxicated with glee, he danced about the foot of the cross, howling curses and damnations. Blasphemes, vile and unmentionable, filled the air.

"Draw near, my mother!

"Now, Carpenter, invite my mother into your

breast. Embrace her full, and find that she is breathlessness. Drink her venom and know that *she* is that lie who lied to all mankind. Then shall you come to me and find your peace in me, for I am your grave."

"Father," whispered Jesus. "Oh, Eternal Spirit, you with whom I have spent eternity, you who entered Mary and became my presence, you who formed me in the likeness of human flesh, yet kept me ever one with thy Holy Spirit, I bid thee, Eternal Spirit, *depart from me.*

"Forsake my spirit, flee this wretched place, for I who became God incarnate must now become Sin incarnate. Return, O Holiness, to our eternal home. Unless you leave, Sin cannot come. Turn from me as I become all abomination. Close your ears to my mindless cries as I drink the cup. For by your departure and Sin's entrance surely shall my soul be blind and its presence drive me into madness.

*Forsake me now, my Father,*
*even as the cup is passed to me.*
*Then, Father, reach back into that distant past,*
*before the ages,*
*when I was the slain Lamb.*
*Let that moment wed this earthly hour.*
*Join them both in me*
*here upon the tree.*
*Let my dying*
*make those two moments*
*into one.*

*Leave me now to destroy*
*Sin*
*even as Sin destroys me.*
*With my final breath*
*shall I thrust this hour*
*into past eternity.*
*Then shall Sin be destroyed*
*before the foundation*
*of creation.*
*I am now lifted up*
*from the earth.*
*I draw all fallen men*
*to a salvation*
*made real even before I created.*
*Oh, so great salvation!*
*Make entrance into time.*

The Carpenter looked out at the whirlwind of iniquity.

"Come, Sin. Come, thou who art the draught within the cup. It is my hour to drink thee full. Come, Sin, make thyself be me."

By that invitation, Sin became a boiling cup.

The Eternal Spirit lifted. Sin swarmed into the bosom of Jesus.

*I have become the fall.*

At that moment Recorder stepped into the heavenlies and found himself beside the Book of

Records. He turned toward the Door. His Lord was
dying.

"I have returned at the moment of the slaying of
the Lamb of God. Must I hear that cry again? Must I
hear the bleating of the Lamb?"

The Lord, now in-wrought with Sin, raised his
head. The cry began.

"Oh!" cried Recorder. "Let this be the final time
I hear this dreadful wail make its way across eternity."

The cry was not unlike the crying of all lambs ever
slain, joining together with all the shrieks of dying
men and screeches of damned demons.

The cry reached its crescendo.

Recorder clutched at his ears.

"Yet once more you will hear," came a voice from
deep inside Recorder's spirit.

"Oh no, no. No. Let this be the last."

The scream continued. Recorder lowered his
hands, raised his head, and for the first time allowed himself to search out the hidden depths of
the cry.

"It is not as before. This time . . . I hear within that
piteous cry . . . the chimes of triumph."

Recorder grabbed at one of the books in his keeping, even the *Record of Sin*. In this book were recorded
the transgressions and misdeeds of all mankind.

Frantically tearing through the pages, Recorder
stared in unbelief at what he saw. The records had
changed. The charges, all of them, laid against every

soul who ever lived . . . records of all acts of unrigh-
teousness and all sins ever committed in all the
ranks of mankind had been commuted. Disappeared.

"Altered! All of them changed! Nay, vanished. All
charges are now laid to one man only: Jesus Christ,
the Lamb of God."

# CHAPTER
## *Thirty-Two*

"Take me now, Death. I have become Sin. Take me as you have taken all others. But as you come, forget not that all the charges of unholiness against creation now reside in me alone. As I slip into that grave which you so long designed to be mine, know that Sin will be entombed with me."

"Of what matter is this? It is only that you die and I be god," answered the angel of death.

"You must hold me three days, Azell. *That* is your final battle. Only then are you my conqueror and I your prey."

Death roared with laughter. "I will hold you, not *three* days, but *forever.*"

"You know not all things, Death."

Death blazed in anger.

"You spoke those same words to me at your throne when first I came into your creation. In Egypt one of your angels defied me with these same words. I am through with this gibberish. I need not know all. I need only to know you belong to me, and no power can set you free!"

Azell lunged at the Carpenter.

Life and Death collided. For an instant creation vanished as Light and Darkness succumbed to one another. Then did those two final foes begin to slip into the cross.

> *Thy sting, Death. Press full*
> *thy sting in me.*
> *Do thy bidding, and mine.*

"I am your shroud. The grave is my victory over you. I and my mother strangle you. Together we kill. Receive now your wage, O Life."

"My body and soul are yours, frail Death. Hold me if you can."

The Carpenter, who long ago had chosen that his last breath would reveal his deepest Mystery, spoke one last time.

"This is what you do not know! There was death before you came, Azell."

"I know *all* dying, Carpenter. There was not death before I came," sneered Azell.

"There was an age before the ages. Of that age you know nothing! It was the age *before* creation. In that age, long before you, *I died!* I died before I created."

> *Death, thou art a fool.*
> *Thou, Death, art but my servant.*
> *To think thyself more*
> *is but to be the greater fool.*

*Take me to thy chambers.*
*There in thy domain*
*shall I set light*
*and awaken to life*
*the slumbering ones.*
*Then in those vaults*
*shall there be revealed that*
*all those whom thou didst call dead*
*do but sleep.*
*None die*
*except one.*
*Thou art well named,*
*for, Death, thou alone shall die.*
*All others awake*
*at my bidding.*
*Death, thou art too proud.*
*Thou knowest not even who thou art.*
*For thou art not*
*Death.*
*More frail than sleep art thou.*
*Thou art nought*
*but my dark disguise.*
*Wouldst thou meet true Death, Azell?*
*I am Death,*
*not thee.*
*In thy chambers*
*learn what thou didst not know.*
*Death, I now be Death to thee.*
*I thy dying*
*be.*

Jesus threw his head against the tree and cried out in words baptized in triumph.

> *Azell, this too, you did not know.*
> *Before I created all things,*
> *I finished all things!*

Panic ripped across the face of Death as he felt himself plunging inside a vortex beyond his understanding. Writhing and shrieking, Death disappeared into the breast of the Carpenter.

Suddenly the scene changed again. Golgotha reentered time and space. The hill above Jerusalem was again in full view.

It was 6:00 P.M.

The last words spoken to Azell, outside creation, now thundered in triumph across the vaults of the universe as an age before the ages made itself one with space and time. Two cries, one unleashed on Golgotha and the other before creation, joined and became one.

*IT IS FINISHED.*

# CHAPTER
## Thirty-Three

Thousands of pilgrims who had milled about the temple courtyard all day now pressed their way toward the temple entrance. Even those who were on Golgotha's high slopes turned toward the temple doors.

"It is their Passover," observed one of the guards.

Dramatically the high priest appeared before the temple's entrance. As he did, he raised the paschal lamb above his head for all to see. Then, turning away from the onlooking masses, he reentered the temple. The Passover had begun.

At that very moment a terrible scream bugled forth from one of the hills above the city. All eyes turned toward Golgotha.

The cry resounded across the earth, winged its way into the past and future, then rose to find its way even into the eternals.

"The Galilean. He dies."

The earth began to shake. "Earthquake!" many began to cry.

Unknown to mortals, the epicenter of that earthquake was beneath the temple's altar.

The reverberations grew violent. The temple itself began to groan and reel, a victim of some subterranean conflict. The foundation of the ancient temple, its ancient altar and its new facade of gold, were being shaken by the mighty hands of some invisible force.

As suddenly as had come the earthquake, just as suddenly the skies turned into the blackest of black. Within the temple courtyard there remained only the faintest glimmer of light. Joining the darkness came the sound of cracking wood. Timber somewhere in the temple was splintering.

The temple doors ripped from their hinges, and then in an earsplitting roar crashed to the floor.

Fast following that came another sound, that of cloth being shredded.

"Look!" cried one of the priests, straining to see clearly in the dim light. "No, do not look!" cried another. "It is not for us to see what is now exposed."

The vast tapestry hanging in front of the Holy of Holies was shaking furiously as the timber holding it splintered. The earth shook again. The curtain smashed upon the golden floor. The Holy of Holies, not to be seen by the eyes of sinful men, was now exposed.

"Look the other way! Look the other way!" the priests began to scream. "It is forbidden to look upon the holiest of all places."

"Even the eyes of the heathen can see in," wailed one of the priests.

As violent as was this scene, it was eclipsed by a grander event taking place in the heavens at the same moment. Even as earth's eyes watched the torn curtain fall upon the golden floor, celestial eyes turned toward the *Door!*

"Never! The Door *never* trembles!" cried innumerable angels in unison.

The vast, impenetrable entrance into the heavenly sphere, that place which marks the boundary between heaven and earth, was wrenching at its hinges. Heaven's Door and the temple's curtain shook, twisted, and groaned as one. Both wailed in one last contortion. As the curtain fell in Jerusalem's temple, the Door to heavenly places ripped at its hinges and swung open.

"The Boundary!" gasped Exalta. "The Boundary between heaven and earth lies unprotected!"

"What manner of moment is this!" cried Gabriel.

Hinges shattered, the Door collapsed. In its place a gaping hole. An entrance with no door.

Angels froze in dismay.

"The fiery sword!" cried one of the messengers standing near the entranceway. The circling, flaming sword had begun to slow. To the unnerving of angels the sword's violent blaze also went out. The sword then disappeared.

"No!" cried Rathel. "That sword has never ceased to protect this realm."

"The cherubim!" came another frantic voice.

Those terrible creatures, who were terror to all others, found themselves terrified. With no door to protect, their task done, the cherubim flew toward the throne and disappeared into that place from whence they had come so long ago, into the glory of the supernal.

Gabriel rushed to the entrance. "It now is as it was when the garden was on earth and there was un-guarded access between heaven and earth."

It was at that particular moment that Michael, having ended his odyssey with Recorder, appeared beside Gabriel.

"Michael, where have you been?"

"To places of which it is not lawful to speak."

"Behold the Door, Michael! Your sword was never more needed."

Michael's only response was a smile.

Gabriel found himself saying aloud, "Michael, you are sane! Your madness is lifted."

Transfixed by the sight of so gaping a hole, Michael heard not a word Gabriel spoke.

"It is once again as it was the day earth and heaven were joined, is it not Gabriel?"

"Yes. But it also means we who live in the holiest of all places now live in an unguarded realm. Is it possible that the fallen race of earth could make entrance here? What does this mean?"

"It would appear that the death of the Son of God

has made great changes, perhaps making the heavenlies accessible even for . . ."

"For whom?" pressed Gabriel. "For our enemy? For unredeemed man?"

"To whom the Doorway may now be opened, I cannot say," replied Michael.

Then, almost in a chuckle, he continued, "But this I do know. Our problem with an unprotected Doorway has just now begun."

"What?" retorted Gabriel.

"Look!"

"Oh no . . ."

# CHAPTER
## *Thirty-Four*

Exalta and Rathel were standing in the Doorway, deeply engrossed in angelic speculation.

"The gate is ripped off, the cherubim gone, the fiery sword disappeared. All the angels in creation could never fill that hole. Consider it, Rathel: the Door to heaven—*open!*"

Rathel's spirit had leaped beyond the obvious. "The garden could slip through a hole that big," he mused.

"That is not likely. Not as long as—"

"What is that?" asked Rathel.

"I do not know, Rathel. I do not know what that is!"

"Gloir!" cried Exalta, "Look!"

"What is that?" came Gloir's frantic response.

"Rathel, what is that?" repeated Gloir.

"I do not know. But I am frightened. For the first time, ever, I know fear!"

Gloir stepped beside Rathel.

"Did I hear you say . . . ? Rathel, you are trembling all over."

"Exalta, find Michael," demanded Rathel.

"Gloir, should I draw my sword?" continued Rathel.

"Not unless you want it to melt!" The voice belonged to Michael.

"Michael, did you see. . . . What is that?"

At that instant Gabriel appeared. Gloir was stunned to see Gabriel's trumpet raised high above his head.

"Is this the end?" gulped Rathel.

Ignoring Rathel's question, Gabriel only stared down toward earth.

"What is that? *What* is that?"

"We do not know," came the trembling voice of Gloir, "but I believe it is headed this way. Oh, I *really* do believe it is headed this way."

All eyes turned toward Michael's sword. It was sheathed.

"Your sword, Michael?" questioned Rathel.

"I would say it is of no use, Rathel. Would you not agree?"

Rathel did not reply, but only continued staring at Michael's undrawn sword.

"Oh no," moaned Exalta. "It *is* coming this way!"

"What is that? I demand to know," ordered Gabriel to no one in particular.

There was no reply.

"What shall we do? Are we to stand here and do nothing?" continued Gabriel as he turned to face

Michael. "There is no Door. There is no flaming sword, no cherubim."

By now the entire heavenly host was gathered at that space where once had stood a vast protective door.

Gabriel turned his gaze away from the bright blue ball.

"Whatever that is, it is brighter, purer, and holier than anything this angel's eyes have ever seen, save the throne of God."

"Does it have a right to come here?" inquired Adorae.

"We would be wise not to ask if it has a right to be here. Rather we should ask, if it should come into our midst, do we have any right to live in its presence," responded Michael.

After a moment, Gabriel's anxiety reached its limits. As one crying for mercy he called out again, *"What is it?"*

At that moment, Recorder appeared beside Gabriel.

"In the name of all that is holy, Recorder, what is that?"

The face of the ancient messenger was aglow.

"Do not ask *what* it is. Ask, rather, *who* it is."

"You mean that is *someone?* A person? You mean . . . a . . ."

"Not only is it a someone," responded Recorder, "it is a human being!"

"A what?!"

"You heard me, Gabriel, you are not deaf."

"But that is impossible: They do not look like *that!*"

"That which is approaching our realm, our now *unguarded* realm, *is* a human being. Not only a human being but one who was very much one of the fallen race of fallen Adam."

The entire host had surrounded Recorder, hanging on every word. The shared thought in every spirit was, *But who can this be?*

"Such glory. Such beauty, such purity. Such perfection. Never have my eyes seen the like. I have wondered about this moment since first the Book of Life was placed in my charge!"

The sons of light stood in wonder at the sound of Recorder's voice.

Gabriel, both frustrated and frightened, did what no angel had ever done before nor since. Gabriel grabbed Recorder and, shaking him, thundered, "If this is a *who,* then who is it?"

Paying no attention to such irreverence, an ecstatic Recorder threw his hands above his head and roared.

"Do you not know? Host of heaven, have you not understood? Sons of creation, do you not realize what grand a redemption your Lord has this day wrought? Do you not know who even now comes to join us in our realm?"

The face of every angel was blank.

"Then I shall tell you! Go now. Go out to meet

him, for he is the *first* fruit of your Lord's redeeming blood.

"Do you not understand who comes this way, robed in glory, robed in light, robed in perfect righteousness, robed in the very holiness of God?

"He comes into our midst blameless, unindictable, and without reproach.

"He is the first of a great multitude that will some day come to be known as *the holy ones.*

"Look at him. As glory comes toward glory, look at him. See his hands and feet. Just a moment ago he died upon a cross . . . a criminal. Now, by the blood of the Lamb, he is glory beyond glory. Behold, the bedouin!" roared Recorder.

"Behold, the thief! Behold the criminal who died upon a cross! Behold *redemption!*"

Out of pure wonder, awe, and exaltation, the sons of creation unleashed a thunderous shout that almost cracked the vaults of heaven.

"The thief! It is the thief! It is the thief!"

With a quickness reserved only for angels, the heavenly throng poured out of the open portal, forming as they did a glowing procession of light that reached the tip of earth's skies. Shouts of joy and jubilation flooded the air as the bedouin reached the staircase of angels.

> *The thief! The thief!*
> *Comes now the thief*
> *to join us in our realm.*

*By the blood,*
*by the blood*
*of the redeeming Lamb.*

The bedouin, in the meantime, had gone quite berserk with joy, wonder, and believing disbelief. Looking first at his hands and feet, both glowing with light, then backward to watch the receding form of a fallen planet, then above at shouting, incoherent angels.

"I am clothed in purest white. I glow. You up there. You are angels! Yes. That is what you are . . . but how do I know that? Look at me! I am holy! Look at me. I tell you nothing ever looked like I look."

Approaching the first angels, the bedouin continued yelling his wild exuberances.

"Here I come! Here I come! Look at me. Here I come! I see! I see the unseen! I, a creature of the visible realm, can *see* the invisible. . . . Has anyone ever seen the unseen? Look at me. Have you ever seen anything like me? Lord of glories. Father of all. Wait for me. Here I come!"

Having reached the vanguard of the angels, the bedouin began dancing up the stairway of clouds. Angels watched in shock and joy as he grabbed one of the messengers, then hugged and kissed him.

"I was the thief! That was me! I *was* the thief. But not now. I do not know what I am, who I am, or where I am. But I am wonderful! That is what I am. I am wonderful.

"Someone tell me what I am.

"It matters not! I met him. Did you hear me, I who am called Bedouin, I saw him. He died with me, just as he said he would. He came down and died with me. He has redeemed even me!"

Now it was Recorder who spoke, shocking one and all as he rushed out to meet the thief.

"O Bedouin! O Bedouin! I have waited so long to meet you. Hear me, one and all. This thief, his is the *first* name written in the Book of Life. You, Bedouin, are the *first* of the redeemed. Behold, a holy one!"

With that word, not only a thief but an entire realm of heavenly citizens went quite berserk with joy. The spirit of a righteous man made holy, and ten thousand times ten thousand angels, all utterly rapturous, stepped into the paradisial realms, there to await the hour when others robed in like perfection and light would storm their way to glory!

# CHAPTER
## *Thirty-Five*

The Sabbath was over. The first day of the week, a festival day called Firstfruits, was dawning.

While it was still very much the night, one of the temple priests made his way out of the temple into the barley fields, coming eventually to a small field that had markings all around it. It was required of the priest to come to this place, which the Sanhedrin had designated as sacred, and there cut barley sheaves from the grain stalks that had arisen from the soil.

Having carefully sickled the tender stalks, the priest placed them into a basket. Returning to the temple, the priest was subject to a few ritual questions asked each year at this time.

"You have the basket?"

"I do."

"Did you find the grain in a field marked off by the Sanhedrin?"

"I did."

"And did you sickle it properly?"

"I did."

"Then from these firstfruits of the coming harvest we will prepare bread. At the rising of the sun we will celebrate the firstfruits of the harvest."

"It will be a rich harvest this year," reported one of the older priests. "So rich, there is a very good possibility that, in seven weeks, at harvest time, this could become the greatest harvest in memory."

The sheaves were shaken until all the seed had fallen into a waiting pan. Every grain was roasted, not one overlooked. The *fire* touched every seed. Next the grain, now cooked with fire, was crushed, beaten, and sifted until it became fine flour. That done, oil was poured upon the crushed grain.

Finally the priests molded the grain into a loaf of bread and thrust it into a blazing furnace.

"The morning sun will break the horizon any moment. The hour of firstfruits has arrived," announced the designated priest.

Quickly the bread was taken from the furnace and brought into the temple and to the altar of God. Those first seeds to break out of the ground, now become bread, were lifted high above the priest's head and waved before God.

As at the moment of Passover, so again this day, Firstfruits was greeted by a trembling earth. Nothing less than the bowels of the earth *and* the foundations of heaven were in travail.

In the invisible realm, where events are seen and understood far better than on earth, it soon became clear that the universe was suffering a mighty duel, even the final confrontation between Life and Death. Whatever the outcome, creation itself was the prize.

The heavenlies trembled violently. Its survival was not at all a certainty.

# CHAPTER
## *Thirty-Six*

The foundation of the invisible realm groaned in pain. The sapphire pavement cracked, then buckled. Surprised angels found themselves being thrown to their knees while the sound of millions of swords being drawn accompanied their struggle to regain their footing.

"Our final battle?" exclaimed Exalta to Gabriel. "It is the end of the third day."

"It is not our battle. It is the final assay," announced Michael. "Of this we have no part. We can but wait. And hope. Somewhere deep in the bowels of earth, beneath the garden tomb, there rages a battle unlike any that will ever again be known. In a few brief moments Life or Death will be annihilated. Creation hangs in the balance."

Again angels staggered and fell as heaven reeled under another assault. A deafening groan joined the shaking.

"The firmament is in agony," whispered Gabriel. "It may be, in a few moments, we will not exist. No less than the life of God is at risk."

Again fissures ripped across the sapphire floor. The entire cosmos was contorting with a fury surpassing that of the fall.

Once more the foundations of the heavenlies were pounded by a shaking of astonishing proportions. Angels were flung about everywhere. The entire host was in disarray.

"Gabriel!" declared Michael. "Gather all messengers in the unseen realm. Empty the heavens. *Everyone* to the tomb. There we will wait to know either victory or extinction."

"Someone must stay!" responded Gabriel.

"That is my charge. Now quickly, to the tomb."

"Michael, you must not stumble," warned Gabriel.

Michael was about to answer when there came a strange flash of black nothingness.

"We witnessed this only twice before. When Death first appeared before the throne of God, and then again just three days ago when Death slipped into Sheol with Jesus. This may signal the end."

Creation flashed into nothingness again.

"Death is winning," muttered Gabriel.

Once more the strange blank of nothingness enveloped the heavens, only this time longer.

"We have disappeared! If, within this battle, Azell wins, neither we nor creation will reappear!"

Again creation vanished momentarily, this time longer still.

"Death has the upper hand," whispered Michael.

"Azell will not let him go. The battle between our Lord and Azell is at its zenith."

Once more a flicker. Then the heavens disappeared. Then again. And again. "We vanish, then reappear. How long?" queried Gabriel. "Is Death his equal?"

Heaven's foundations trembled again.

"Everyone, out of our realm! We are useless here, we are useless on earth," shouted Gabriel.

"To the tomb. Gather at the tomb, all of you," he commanded in a voice that swept across the entire sphere.

Instantly the unseen realm was emptied of all messengers save one.

The slamming upheavals rose in fury. Michael tried valiantly to stay on his feet, but with every passing second his efforts became more evidently in vain.

Another jolt. The sundering of the heavenlies was everywhere. The unseen realm thundered in echoing cracks and deafening groans. Michael found himself sailing across the sapphire pavement. Only by thrusting his sword hard into heaven's floor was he able to maintain his balance.

"My knees must not buckle," he commanded.

Creation blinked again, its return coming ever so slowly, its light much dimmer now. There was no doubt, Death had almost won.

*It is the end of the heavens,* thought Michael. *Shall*

*Death rule over an abyss of nought where even graves do not exist?*

Once more Michael was hurled across the sapphire pavement. "The heavens cannot possibly withstand another such tremor. It will surely crumble. There must be a place somewhere in creation where I can maintain my footing. Yet *everything* is disintegrating!"

In the midst of the barest of light, revelation broke upon Michael's spirit. "All that is created is shaken. But there is a place where—"

Michael flashed his way across the heavens crying, "To the throne."

While everything around him twisted, ripped, and collapsed, Michael lunged toward the throne room. Just as he was about to crumble to the floor, he reached the footstool of the throne. Michael sheathed his sword and roared in defiance to Death.

"Here will I stand, before the throne! *The unshakeable throne.*"

As in response, there was another deafening roar. Creation blinked again and disappeared, this time returning ever so slowly and ever so dim.

"Never . . . before . . . so . . . dim. For a certainty the next convulsion will tell."

Another vanishing of creation. Much shorter. It was followed by a howl, unlike anything even an archangel might believe possible.

This was followed by a final blink of creation.

The shaking ended. Light did not return. Michael felt himself disappearing into the black, blank void.

In the darkness there arose a cry. Its words were indiscernible, but it was an unmistakable cry of triumph!

"But who is victor?" Michael called aloud.

The cry of triumph, born in the bowels of the earth, had billowed its way across earth and was now ascending heavenward.

"Such a cry will, of itself, destroy all! It is a sound unlike anything I have ever heard before."

At that moment the deafening cry reached heaven's open portal.

"The voice—who speaks? The victor—who?"

Then . . . light! Brighter than angels' eyes have ever seen nor dreamed.

"That light, I know it. That voice, I know it, too! It is the voice of the Carpenter!

"The cry is his!

"O Lord of all, your thundering is so great I cannot understand your words."

Then it came, ripping its way into the vaults of heaven.

*I AM VICTOR OVER DEATH!*

Blinded in light, deafened by a shout of ultimate victory, there was only one thing for Michael to do, one place for him to be. The tomb!

At a speed never before achieved by any angel,

159

Michael joined an innumerable throng of angels who were encircling the tomb even as the cry of victory continued its triumphant proclamation across the universe.

What ensued was shouting so tumultuous that, in the ages that followed, it was rumored among angels that even the voice of cherubim and seraphim could be heard joining in the exaltation. While a vacant heaven was bathed in the healing light of glory, on earth the citizens of heaven raised praises to their Lord in a bedlam of chaotic joy.

"Death is dead. That serpent Lucifer has lost his fiendish friend," announced Gabriel. "Victory won within the bowels of the earth is about to be revealed within the tomb."

# CHAPTER
## *Thirty-Seven*

All the powers of the Eternal Spirit had come together in one place: the tomb. Out of the inmost portions of the lifeless body of Jesus burst forth a blast of light greater than that which had exploded at the beginning of creation.

Now, from out of that tomb streamed golden fire, and in the midst of this ineffable glory, Light of all lights, even Life Eternal, revealed itself to be a man!

*I am the firstborn from the dead.*
*Nor shall I ever die again.*
*In me my chosen ones also have died.*
*In rising from the womb of death,*
*they—in me—rise with me . . .*
*never to die again.*
*My chosen ones,*
*now glorious ones,*
*are born from the dead.*

"Old creation, now vanish," commanded the Carpenter. "It is not for you to share space with my new creation.

"Come forth, my new creation! You, the new creatures, now in me, come forth with me. Arise as I arise! Ascend when I ascend."

Jesus the Christ—Son of the Living God, his flaming body dazzling gold and white, blazing with fiery light, carrying the redeemed one *in* him—rose from the dead. Passing *through* his graveclothes he stood inside Joseph's tomb robed in glory.

God, incarnate as man, crucified, now risen and about to ascend, triumphant over all, billowing cataracts of torrential light and rivers of fire, roared his victory shout.

*I HAVE RISEN!*

Passing through the stone door, the Lord of all glory stepped out upon the earth, threw up his hands, and shouted greetings to the awaiting sons of light.

Spirits of bright angels broke out in wild delirium of praise.

Rapture reigned.

Celebration became ecstasy.

Chaotic rejoicing and wild ebullience ruled the hour.

Even while grand hysteria roared across the citizens of heaven, the Lord of Death pointed to the tomb.

Two magnificent archangels soared into the air while uncountable millions of angels whirled in streams of sparkling light about the still-sealed tomb.

Michael and Gabriel began a slow descent until their feet touched the earth beside the huge stone door, while the rest of the angelic host shouted one another deaf.

Together Michael and Gabriel rolled back the stone. The tomb was so very, very empty! This was more than angel spirits could contain. Chaos gave way to pandemonium, as enraptured angels shouted praises and sang songs in utter disarray.

Praise, cheers, and shouts rose one above the other from the throats of angels quite delirious.

After what came to be the greatest display of praise in all angelic history, disheveled messengers finally found a semblance of composure and began to sing triumphantly.

*Risen,*
*yes, risen!*
*Risen above all!*
*Risen, yes, risen,*
*far above all!*
*Nought else*
*can reach him.*
*Heaven's roof*
*'neath him falls.*
*He is exalted*
*so far above all.*

163

And when angels' voices could no longer shout nor sing nor even whisper, mute citizens of heaven fell at the sacred feet of the Most High Lord and worshiped him.

CHAPTER
# Thirty-Eight

"There is a room in Jerusalem, locked and bolted," said the Lord to his gathered angels.

"Come, we will visit this room where ten frightened men are hiding. Men who do *not* believe in the Resurrection! I desire that every angelic eye see what is about to take place within that room. This morning you were with me at the entrance of the tomb. You also beheld what happened within the heart of a woman named Mary Magdalene. You witnessed her spirit raised from the dead. You witnessed my Spirit become one with . . ." The Lord paused.

"Tonight I will meet those ten frightened men face-to-face. When I do, I will allow angelic eyes to see that which the eyes of God see."

Michael raised his hand. So likewise did Gabriel. Instantly the heavenly host stepped through the open Door and out upon the cobbled streets of Jerusalem. In a nearby house the former disciples of the Carpenter huddled together, speaking to one another in hushed whispers.

"Rumors. I do not care what you say. It is only rumors." Levi was speaking.

"Mary Magdalene does not lie. She never has. It has been her honesty that has undone us on so many an occasion," insisted John.

"No, she does not lie, but I think she has been seeing things that are not there."

"Then explain what happened today on the Emmaus Road."

"I do not explain it. I just do not believe it."

"I saw the empty tomb," remonstrated John.

Peter nodded his head in agreement but added gravely, "But if this is all we have, or ever will have, we shall spend the rest of our lives doubting, or at least wondering . . . while, at other times, believing. One way or the other, let us hope we soon learn more than we know now. Presently I know only enough to spend the rest of my life in confusion."

"There is one thing that burns in my mind," continued John. "If he really rose, if Mary Magdalene has reported his words accurately, then there is a mystery here."

The eyes of nine men narrowed on John.

"What mystery?"

"Today the Magdalene reports that he used a word he has never used before."

"What word?"

"He used the word *brothers*. Never before has he called us brothers."

"So?"

"Listen to me. There is not a man in this room who has the seed of Jesus' ancestors in him. In this room there is no one who shares a hereditary relationship to him."

John's words were followed by a silence finally broken by a question.

"John, you are not implying . . . ?"

"I am implying nothing. I am but *wondering.* Nonetheless, I have to tell you something. The words he spoke to us during these last three years, they have been coming back to me in a flood. I am remembering so much. And I understand everything in a new, deeper way. Much of what he said I am understanding for the first time."

"Yes, the same is true for me," volunteered each man.

"If he has actually risen, if he is really out there somewhere walking around on this earth, if he really has been victorious over death, if divine Life inhabits his being . . . if God the Father really indwelt him all these years, then . . . well . . . it is possible that he could plant the Life of the Father in . . . in . . . others. *Then,* and only then, would we share the same seed! Then might he not call us *brothers,* and be correct in his words?"

"The Life of God inside man? That is absurd."

"Oh? Was the Life of God inside of Jesus an absurdity? Personally, I believe the Father dwelt within him. Perhaps his Life can never dwell inside of us. Perhaps. But what causes me to doubt my disbelief is that I keep remembering his words, when he said . . ." John paused.

Some kind of presence had entered the room.

Ten men, already very frightened, became more frightened still.

"Do any of you . . . *I feel his presence,*" whispered Peter.

Ten disciples froze like statues.

John dared breathe. "I would know that feeling anywhere. His *presence* is in this room."

"Yes," breathed a terrified Matthew.

"It is his ghost. It is here!"

John looked toward the barred door. James let out a gasp and fell backward against the wall. Peter, too terrified to move, forced himself to raise his head.

"If it is the ghost of Jesus, oh, pity our poor souls. It is the ghost of the Teacher."

"Peace," came a voice.

There was no way to mistake that voice.

# CHAPTER
## *Thirty-Nine*

A man can push himself against a stone wall just so far and no farther. But the men in that room had forgotten that, as they removed themselves as far as possible from the figure that had appeared in the middle of the room.

A smile broke across the face of the one whom they hoped was the Lord, but equally feared that he was.

"Are you frightened? Your hearts are doubting? Peter, do you see this hand? James, look at my feet." In horror James looked.

"Do you see where the nails tore my flesh? A ghost does not have such things."

Not one man among them could find his voice.

"Look carefully." The Lord pulled back his robe.

"There, in my side. A scar."

Several of the disciples had begun murmuring prayers, others were crying, while yet others were shaking fitfully. Peter, his head and neck pressed hard against the wall, was biting his hand. Even John could not move.

"Do you see my side?" asked the Lord again. With terrified eyes every disciple looked toward his wounded side.

"It is him. It is Jesus." John began to cry.

"I do not believe it," stammered Peter, bursting into tears.

Still, not one man moved toward his Lord. Rather, they began reaching out and grabbing one another, holding each other furiously. Still no one removed himself from the wall.

Jesus looked about.

"Is there anything here to eat?"

His words were almost more than they could bear. He spoke so normally, so casually. That lack of pretense which they had come to love in him was echoing in the room and in their hearts. His presence was now an exotic aroma.

Simon reached out, picked up a piece of boiled fish, retrieved a honeycomb, and then, in what could only be described as a mingling of horror and glee, pushed a plate toward his Lord. The Carpenter smiled and nodded.

It was more than the human heart could bear.

*Let me die here, now, in joy and gladness, so that I might not have to speak to him of what happened that awful night* was the thought that filled Peter's mind.

Jesus picked up the plate. Ten men gasped.

He could actually hold the plate. It did not fall to the floor! They watched mesmerized as he took the honey and fish in his hand and began to eat.

"It is not a ghost," stammered Simeon.

Jesus began looking slowly around the room, his eyes finally coming to rest on Peter.

"Peace to you."

Still no one moved.

At that particular moment the risen Son of the Living God raised one hand.

In the eyes of onlooking angels, earth vanished. Only the room was there, suspended in the eternals. The eyes of angels could see nothing but a room of ten men now standing before the Christ. All else had disappeared.

Jesus walked over to Simon Peter.

# CHAPTER
## *Forty*

"It is true," whispered Michael in wonder. "It is really true! He is really going to do it! First the thief came into our midst. Then Mary Magdalene met her Lord at the tomb. There he planted his very Life in her. Now the ten deserters, even the cursing, denying fisherman. Has grace ever known such boundlessness?"

What no eyes but God's can see now became the venue of angels, for they were being invited to view Peter as God saw Peter. What first they beheld was Peter's body . . . as God sees it. It was corrupted beyond all telling.

"Our Lord has not made provision to save human flesh," whispered Michael. "I must therefore believe that if he has given up on the corrupted body of man, if it is outside the pale of salvation, then it must be that he plans to *replace* it. A glorified body, not unlike his own, for those who believe. Ah, now that would be grace!"

Still the angels gazed. The soul of Simon Peter suddenly came into sharp focus. For an instant Peter's soul appeared . . . black and filthy, not too unlike that hideous gathering of sin that came to the cross. But that sight abruptly changed. Peter's darkened soul was being touched by something that was crimson red.

"Surely, the blood of the Lamb," intoned Gloir.

In the blink of an eye the soul of Peter became as white as the whitest snow.

Some angels watched this unfolding drama in silent awe. Others wept. But all stained their faces with tears.

The spirit that was in Peter, recessed deep down in the inmost part of his soul, gradually came into view. Angels' tears began to glisten like fire. At first Peter's spirit was almost indistinguishable from his soul, but as time passed it became evident that there was a difference. His soul, only a moment ago still part of the tragic fall, was now redeemed. His spirit, on the other hand, still lay dormant and functionless.

Exalta gave voice to angelic thought. "That spirit in Peter came from our realm. That spirit, if it were alive to the spiritual world, could hear, or at least *sense*, the voice of God. If that spirit were alive, it would be a place where Peter could make his home. He could enter there, and live there. More. If his spirit were alive, then the Life of God would have a rightful place of habitation . . . within Peter."

"If only that spirit were alive," agreed Rathel, "Oh, what glory that would be. We would once more

174

share commonality with man. Both of us would have living spirits."

"Man would once more be a citizen of *two* realms," came the shaking voice of Gabriel.

"Our Lord has risen from the dead. He has conquered death. Totally. Utterly. Completely. Death has no power over him. At his word Death vanishes," added Gloir.

With that Exalta began speaking, but in his rapture he was completely incoherent.

"Quiet, Exalta," urged Adorae.

But Exalta knew that he knew something. Most inappropriately, he cried out at the unfolding scene. "Lord, you can raise Peter's spirit from the dead! You can, Lord. You can. I know you can!"

Every angel turned and stared at Exalta, then shook their heads in dismay at his unseemly outburst.

"Raise him, Lord!" cheered Exalta, almost unable to contain himself.

"Overtalkative messenger," grumbled Rathel.

But on the face of him who *is* Resurrection, there broke a smile.

Angels watched spellbound as a whirlwind of the holy breath churned about in the Lord's deepest being.

"He *really* is letting us see as he sees!" breathed Gabriel.

"Yes, he is quite good at that," agreed Michael.

The Lord's own spirit began to glow within him.

The moment was so much like that wonderful day long ago when a creating Lord breathed something of the heavenly realm into Adam.

"He is going to do it!" cried Exalta.

By now Jesus' spirit glowed like a golden flame. The divine wind of God whirling about inside Jesus began to flow out of him.

The Lord moved toward Simon Peter. Peter watched transfixed as his Lord began, from out of his inmost being, to breathe into Peter the very Life and Spirit of the divine.

Speaking directly to Simon Peter's dead spirit, the Lord commanded, "Receive."

The angels gasped . . . then cheered.

Fiery glory broke forth within Peter. The dormant spirit of Simon Peter had burst into life. Peter's spirit was raised from the dead!

"I knew it," cried Exalta. "I knew he would!"

*So much like Red Earth before he fell,* thought Gloir. "A human being once more has a living, functioning spirit in him. Do you remember, Rathel? Do you remember when Adam had an unflawed soul and a living spirit?"

Rathel nodded.

"But it is not the same. Before the Great Tragedy, Adam's body was flawless. Peter's is not. Nor was Adam's soul flawed. Peter's is. Nonetheless, thank God, Peter now has not only a cleansed soul but—at last—a resurrected and living spirit."

"Not so quick, Rathel! Your Lord is not finished! If

176

I am right in my surmisal, our Lord is about to do inside Peter something that would make an unfallen Adam *jealous!*"

"Receive . . . the Holy Spirit."

"I knew it!" cried Exalta again.

This time it was no less than Gabriel who was behaving most unangelically. "Peter is about to partake of the Lord's Life. Of *divine* Life!"

The host of heaven was about to break into cheers once more. But as they watched the progress of the Holy Spirit, they fell silent. They were seeing far more than even they expected to see.

The Holy Spirit moved into the resurrected spirit of one Galilean fisherman. Once more the Mystery of all mysteries was glimpsed.

Recorder took his golden pen and wrote in the Book of Records.

*His eternal Purpose unfolds. They are risen from the dead. All of them. Risen, and alive with him.*

Simon Peter's spirit had been fully entered into by the Lord's spirit, then even swallowed up in the glory of that Spirit and of that Life.

Recorder's pen continued.

*Not only an element of heaven, but an alien Life, the highest Life of all, is in Peter. The Holy Spirit and Simon's spirit . . . have become one!*

The eyes of angels had seen many things, the expanses of galaxies and glories of heaven, the creation of Adam, the inauguration of Eve, the miracles of Israel's escape, the magnificence of Bethlehem. Today, they had even seen their Lord rise from the dead. Yet here, before their eyes, was a miracle as grand as angels' spirits could ever grasp.

The Spirit of God and the spirit of a man had ceased to be two and had become *one*.

In that most awesome moment, there rang out the voice of Recorder. "Today we have witnessed the foregleam of his oneness with the redeemed!

"God, one with man. . . . God, one with the redeemed! The end of all marvels.

"Companions of the spirituals," continued Recorder, "Now see the *Mystery* unfold. Behold, his eternal Purpose. Your Lord has made himself one with man's spirit!"

Quite suddenly, as on command, the scene began to change. The walls of the room once more found their shape. The streets of Jerusalem reappeared.

Time ticked again.

# CHAPTER
## *Forty-One*

Simon Peter burst into tears. In unrestrained abandonment he reached out and embraced his Lord.

Nine other men raced forward to their Lord. A small clump of eleven men wept for joy.

As they embraced, repented, were forgiven, and forgave, the Lord began to speak.

*I told you I would go*
*and prepare a place for you,*
*so that where I always am,*
*there you may also come*
*and there always be.*

*I am always with my Father.*
*He in me.*
*I in him.*

*Where I always am,*
*you have never been able to come.*
*Until now.*
*But now!*

*I have done*
*what I have said I would do.*
*I have gone and prepared*
*a place for you.*
*That place is within my Father.*
*Within him*
*are many places to abide.*

*I have told you many times:*
*"I am in the Father.*
*The Father is in me."*
*Now I will tell you*
*that which is new.*
*Today I am in you*
*and you are in me.*

*Now, my brothers,*
*I have breathed into you*
*my very being.*
*You have my Life.*
*The highest of all the lives that abides in heaven*
*is in you.*
*I am that highest Life.*

*I am in you.*
*I am one with you.*
*You are one with me.*
*As I live by the Father's Life,*
*so, now, you—one with my Life—*
*will draw from my Life.*

*As I live by the Life of my Father,*
*you now live by my Life.*

*By means of my Life alone*
*can you possibly carry out*
*your daily living.*

*This night*
*you are captured in me.*
*And I am captured in you.*

*Never forget my words.*
*Even as I am in you*
*and you are in me . . .*
*remember also that*
*I am in the Father.*
*But because you are in me*
*and I am in you,*
*and I am in the Father,*
*you, therefore, are also in the Father*
*and the Father is also in you.*

*For this was I sent*
*into the world . . .*
*that we might be one.*

# EPILOGUE

"Did you know that the Garden of Eden has changed?" Michael asked Recorder, a note of profound excitement in his voice. "The garden is becoming a—"

"Yes," interrupted Recorder. "I know. But not entirely changed. The Tree of Life is still there. The River of Living Water is still there. The gold and the pearl and the costly stone—they too are still there. Yet, it is true, the garden has ceased to be a garden."

In a hushed whisper Michael continued. "Recorder, the garden has become what Abraham sought but never found. More, the bedouin lives there, and now others. Daily the redeemed arrive, shining forth in their glory like the most costly stones."

"The cross and the tomb have changed many things," responded Recorder. "Be it a garden or be it what it has become, from before the beginning our God intended it to be a habitat—a habitat for the unfallen race of the sons and daughters of God. It has become, well, the habitat of the holy ones. Only its *location* is still out of proper order."

"Is it possible, Recorder—"

"That we might see it slip out of the heavenlies

and once again join the two realms together again?" inserted Recorder.

"It is hard *not* to wonder," said Michael longingly.

"This is all I know," mused Recorder. "Now that the Doorway is open, there is certainly space enough for such an event. As immense as the garden was, nonetheless there is room. I agree, one must wonder."

"God and man strolling together again beside the River of Living Water. Man standing before the Tree of Life . . ." Overcome by the very idea, Michael fell silent.

Then, in a pensive mood, Michael began again. "For a thousand years they observed two festivals that were only a shadow of reality. But now Passover and Firstfruits are a reality. In a few days they will observe another festival that is but a symbol of a coming reality. I cannot help but wonder if, in a few days, we will see the Festival of Weeks also fulfilled.

"And then there is, of course, the Festival of Ingathering."

"Michael, let me read to you what I have, this day, entered into the Book of Records."

*I, Recorder, have witnessed the birth of creation. I have seen the bright blue ball drop from my Master's fingertip. I wept at the fall, stood transfixed at the deluge, cheered as a million souls escaped Egypt, and reveled in the earthen birth of the eternal Son. Then also did I see my Lord and Creator die on Mount Moriah.*

*That tragedy turned to unutterable joy, for I
witnessed the fallen creation die upon the cross. Then,
on this first day of the week, I witnessed Sin and Death
forever conquered!*

*I bear witness to this also: I have seen my Lord rise
from the dead. Triumphant over all things. And I
glimpsed the chosen ones rise in him as he rose.*

*Today I realize that the heaven and earth must no
longer be called creation but henceforth must be known
as the first creation. I stood dumbfounded as I
witnessed my Lord bring forth a new creation, even the
oneness of God's Spirit with man's spirit. A biologically
new, unique species now walks upon the earth. Could I
ever have believed I would witness the birth of two
creations! An old one and a new one. Each is so
different from the other. This new creation, composed
not of the eternals nor of matter and time, but a
creation composed of that which is the nature, Life,
and being of God.*

Recorder looked up. Michael was silent.

"Now, Michael, I shall make one last entry con-
cerning these matters. Hear what it is I pen.

*There remains at least one more day as awesome as
creation, as wondrous as the Resurrection and even
today's beginning of a new creation. What awaits us
out there may well be the most cataclysmic event that
created eyes shall ever see.*

"What event could that possibly be?" asked Michael, his brow furrowing.

Recorder dipped his fiery golden pen in flaming golden ink, then placed into the records two words:

*The Return*